GUNNER

NORTHERN GRIZZLIES MC BOOK 3

M. MERIN

Gunner: Northern Grizzlies MC (Book 3)

ISBN: 9781982989859

Cover Art by Madelene Martin www.madbookdesigns.com

Edited by Edits by Erin

Formatting by Dark Water Covers

Published in the United States of America.

GUNNER

CHAPTER ONE

RILEY

SITTING IN THIS POINTLESS CLASS WAS PARTICULARLY wretched today. I had gotten my period during my earlier English class, spotting my white jeans and causing endless amusement to those around me as some jock had loudly pointed it out. I never attended high school, but imagine that's what it felt like. I never attended grade school either.

My parents would have packed me off to boarding school if it wasn't for my gram. At the end of the day, she still holds the purse strings to grandfather's trust and that was where their allegiance began and ended. Having a child to appease her, so original.

Gram demanded that I be raised at home, so they compromised with tutors for homeschooling because there was no way they considered the local public school acceptable. Mother seemed to have forgotten it was her alma mater...

Tutors, plural, since mother despised how attached I was to my first one. Ms. Betty was slightly older than mother and

I adored her. Having been pushed aside by my parents I was starved for affection. Gram is wonderful, but she has her own life and routine. I would stay at her house every Friday night growing up and I loved every minute of it.

I once made the mistake of asking gram to let me live with her. I was five or six and she must have questioned me further. I remember her and mother screaming at each other the next day, but most of all I remember my mother slapping me when we got home, then my collarbone was broken when she grabbed my arm to pull me to my room.

I should have learned my lesson then.

I didn't, and my eighth birthday was the last day I ever saw Ms. Betty. She had made the grievous error of showing up with a birthday present and balloons for me; as neither mother nor father had added my birthday to their calendars, they were unaware of the day. After that, my tutor was switched out about every year.

Shaking my head to clear old memories, I slip my sweater off to wrap around my waist during a bathroom stop to assess the damage. Still, I was caught off guard by the number of snickers I heard upon entering class. Surely not everyone knew about my period already?

So here I sit. In a class that will not matter to my degree in eight months and two weeks. That is the exact amount of time until I turn eighteen. At that point, I can change my major from the parental units' imposed and enforced pre-med coursework, to Computer Info Systems. Luckily, the university requires similar core criteria for both majors and with electives needed, I was able to get a few programming classes in already. Not enough to raise any eyebrows when my report card was emailed to the parents, but baby steps...

At the end of the hour, I rush out of class, hoping that my workout bag is in the back seat of my SUV. Sweats aren't optimal but I do not have time to drive home and back in the two hours between now and my last class of the day. Surprised by the number of people gathered near the parking lot, spring or not, it's still chilly today. I dart around the last car and see my SUV.

They weren't all laughing at the blood spot on my jeans. Now, I really wish that was it.

In big black letters, someone wrote "JAILBAIT" along the side of my white Jeep Liberty.

I stumble as I see it. I don't know how I manage to stay on my feet. All my blood has rushed to my face and I am about to burst into tears. My backbone returns when I hear the first giggle, but I will not give them the satisfaction of seeing me wilt.

I will myself to keep walking and try to still the shaking that threatens to overcome my body. Afternoon class be damned.

I drive slowly through campus and then gun it once I'm past the gates. Ten minutes outside of school, I pull over. I cannot go home. They cannot see this. I start to shake in earnest as I pull out my cell. Looking for directions to the closest "do it yourself" car wash, my tears start to fall. Jail-bait, really?

One time, the *one* time, I was determined to feel like an actual teenager was my seventeenth birthday. There was a frat party that a freshman in my chemistry class told me about and as my parents were still in Boise, I made plans to meet her and her friends to go. My parents ended up getting home that night and, with my car missing from the garage, they tracked my phone.

I had been nursing some sort of punch, not that it had any juice in it, since arriving at the party. The girls I met up with had more to drink and we all started dancing. For the first time I felt alive. Having been so isolated from others my age for years, it was an awakening. Especially when a guy reached an arm out to pull me in for a dance. I don't remember much about him, just very average but he wasn't too grabby where he shouldn't be touching, so I stayed in his arms.

Then the yelling started and the music cut off. My parents had arrived. My father, the lawyer, started yelling about *contributing to the delinquency of a minor* and *molestation*. He looked at me and pointed at the door. Following me out they started yelling about how I had shamed them, then he continued it the whole way home, while mother followed behind us in my SUV.

It was the beginning of this semester and the last time any of my classmates talked to me on purpose.

Snapping out of my musings in time to make the turn that the GPS was yapping about, I drive down a few more blocks to get to the car wash. I've lived in Rowansville my whole life but have never been to this part of town. There were random businesses scattered between empty-looking buildings and lots. The attendant on duty at the car wash merely smirks when he sees my SUV before heading back into his office. Driving past him to the furthest stall, I get out and start trying to figure out how this set up works.

A half an hour later I am pretty sure I'd made it worse. Finally giving in to my anger and hurt, I sink to the wet ground against the car, tears streaming down my face and sobs ripping through me. As my breathing calms, I open my eyes to the ground in front of me and see an extraordinary large pair of black leather boots.

Slowly looking up the body in front of me, past dirty jeans topped with a dark t-shirt and a leather vest stands the largest, scariest man I have ever seen. He is humongous, with shaggy brown hair and a smoothly shaved face that has a large scar running down half of it. He's standing over me with a massive scowl on his face. All I can think is he can't be real.

Surprise lights up his face as he removes his sunglasses to reveal startling blue eyes, without removing the cigarette from his mouth he says, "I am."

Gulp. Did I say that out loud?

GUNNER

Not a good day for this shit. I've got furniture projects piled up that need to get done and then Vice called, needing me to run around to a few of the Club's businesses to pick up our cash share for the month. The date for one of our less than legal operations had been moved up and we need the cash sooner rather than later.

Middle of the day on Tuesday looks deader than shit at the car wash, one vehicle parked near the end with no one working on it. Going into the office, Eddie was just closing the safe as I entered.

"Hey man, glad you're here," he leads off, while I light up a smoke.

I hate this slimy asshole and am pretty sure the feeling is mutual, so I can't imagine what's happened, but I grunt and reach out for the bag he's holding.

I flip through it to start the count, expecting silence to get this done quickly but he jumps back in.

"See, there's this girl here and she's like crying or some shit. What do I do? How do I get rid of her?" He asks.

"You bring your little side piece to work and think I give two shits if there's fallout?" I say, separating out the piles.

He starts in again but I hold up my hand so I can get the

count done. Last I'd heard Eddie was trying it with his baby mama again.

I nod as I finish the count and turn to go, he starts again. "It ain't like that, Gunner. She drove in that SUV over there. Some graffiti on the side, she was cleaning it but then she stopped and I heard her crying. SUV said JAILBAIT so I don't want to go near her. Ya know, 'cause Jessica or one of her friends could drive by and see me talking to another girl."

Fuck. I really don't need this bullshit.

Heading back to my bike, I secure the take, light a new smoke with the old one, and mount up fully planning to ride out. Then I hear a low sob and I pause, pointing the bike in her direction and knowing it's a bad idea. I turn the bike off in front of her SUV and walk around it.

The girl is sitting on the wet ground with her knees pulled into her chest, arms wrapped around them and her head tucked down. Shoulder length brown hair obscures her face but her uneven breathing bothers me. Why, I don't know.

I stand there, letting her get it out. Someone had indeed tagged her SUV with the word JAILBAIT and she hadn't gotten much further than smearing the first few letters around.

A moment later she sniffles and slowly raises her head. Fuck. She is beautiful. High cheekbones, perfect ivory skin, a slightly crooked nose, and full peach lips. Her eyes are hidden under long lashes but even from here I can see how red and puffy they are. As her eyes drift up my body, eventually taking in my face, I get my first glance of her eyes and, swollen or not, am taken aback not just by the amber color but by the pain I see within them.

Finally understanding the expression of an old soul, the

only other place I have seen such pain is the battlefield. This is not about her car, her sobs had been built up over years and in this moment, looking down at her, I know she is too young and too good to have felt that type of pain and I will not allow it to stand.

"You can't be real," she says after staring at me intently.

I'm thinking the same thing. "I am."

Her mouth drops open and she blushes. She'd really blush if she knew what I was picturing stuffed in that warm opening.

FUCK. I tense up as my eyes jump back to the word on the SUV.

"How old are you?" I can't stop the anger in my voice, making her eyes widen before narrowing and suddenly looking more angry than defeated. Interesting...little girl has a backbone. "Sorry, it's just, uh," I hold my hand out to her to help her stand. She ignores it, standing on her own and turning to go.

"Wait. I know someone who can fix that. May take a few hours though," I say before thinking. Rewarded by the hopeful look in her eyes, I smile and introduce myself. "Gunner Sorenson."

She smiles shyly and says "I'm Riley," as she sticks her hand out to me. I take her hand and holding it longer than is acceptable, I smile as she quickly shifts her gaze down and away from mine. "And I'm seventeen, hence..." she points to her newly decorated ride, while slowly removing her hand from mine.

"Follow me, I'll get this taken care of," I say, turning back to my bike. I stop when I hear her chuckle behind me. "What's got you smiling, Sweetheart?" I ask, over my shoulder.

With laughter still in her voice, "That was very 'Terminator' of you! Except you're a lot bigger than he is!"

Smiling back, I flick my cigarette away as I get on my bike, "I'm not exactly saving your life here, Sweetheart."

"Today it kind of feels that way," she responds quietly, getting in and starting her SUV.

Damn, if I don't feel even bigger now.

CHAPTER TWO

GUNNER

HEADING A COUPLE MILES OVER TO THE SHOP, I AM KICKING myself. I have to let Vice know I'll be delayed a bit. Shit, I can't just leave her there while I run around. Not one of us would touch a minor, there's plenty of legal pussy, but I just don't want her to be alone.

Checking my mirror, she's still following a car length behind and I start to get nervous she'll peel off, rethinking her decision to follow a 6'8" scar-faced, tattooed stranger through town. Mentally willing her to stick with me, I carefully use my blinkers as we make the final couple turns to the garage.

Turning in behind me, she seems to hesitate in her car, so I quickly stride over to reassure her. "Just stay here for a minute, let me talk to the guys and get you right in. Okay?" I nearly plead through her opened window.

She's biting her lower lip, but nods. Staring at her lips a moment longer than necessary, I turn and head inside.

Connal and Probie are each on separate projects and

from the way it looks in here, I can tell I'll owe them big for helping her out.

"Hey Connal, I need some help," I yell over the music pounding throughout the room. Probie rolls out from under an Oldsmobile to acknowledge me, while Connal looks up from his project.

"Gunner, what's up?" He says, straightening up and reaching for a rag.

"Remember that paint you got off our crash truck after the rally a few years back? This is time sensitive and pretty much the same thing." Seeing him start to shake his head, I quickly throw out, "I'll owe you both for this. I mean it. But it's gotta get done now."

Looking past me towards Riley who's still sitting in her SUV, Connal lets out his breath and asks, "How bad is it?"

"Come on, but hey, see the girl? She's a little sensitive right now and you can't say anything or laugh at it. Got me?" I say, glaring down at him so he knows I'm serious as shit about this. After his quizzical look and nodded agreement, I turn to head back out to Riley.

Probie rolls back out from under the Olds and starts to follow us. Ignoring my glare he pipes in, "Yeah, now I gotta see this."

Rounding the driver's side, Connal mumbles "Shit." As the new addition to the Jeep becomes obvious. Riley steps out, nodding in Connal and Probie's direction, her eyes dance back to me and she asks, "Can it be cleaned off? I just really have to be home tonight."

Connal has continued straight to the graffiti and takes over, "When did this happen?"

"Like three hours ago? I'm not sure, really, I was in class. I tried to, well..." Riley points at her failed attempt at scrubbing it off, her eyes snapping back to me as I knock Probie upside the head. Fucker took one look at the SUV and the girl then started staring at the sky like he'd never seen it before. I shrug and smile at her. She instantly rewards me with a warm smile. "She's seventeen." I say more to myself than them, "Riley, give your keys to Connal here."

As she starts to hand the keys over to Connal, I go for them instead not wanting her to touch him. Tossing them to him and keeping possession of her hand, I start to take her to the office.

"Wait! I need my bags!" Pulling back and opening the back door she leans in and we all see her other little problem at the same time, but fucking Probie couldn't keep his mouth shut.

"Hey, y'know you bled through your jeans, right?"

What can only be described as a wail comes from Riley right about the same time Connal and I simultaneously turn on Probie. I slug him in the gut as Connal bellows at him. Turning, I reach around for Riley, determined to keep a hold of her this time. She follows me, running to keep up, as I lead her to the back office, that has a private bathroom.

"Stay in here, I'll be back in an hour or so." I start to back out but the sight of another tear escaping her gorgeous eyes stops me in where I am. Reaching out to cup both sides of her face I slide my thumbs up her tear tracks, absorbing them. She starts to step closer to me, but closing my eyes and exhaling her scent I gently push her away. The word JAILBAIT is right on the money.

I leave her standing there to go finish my rounds and get the money to Vice. I briefly check in with Connal who has moved the SUV inside and is working with some solvent to remove the tag, I get going so I can get back to her.

I never saw this coming. I know I've never met a girl like her. I am so fucked.

RILEY

Gunner just is super-sized. Not fat but bulky, tall and solid. The moment his huge hands cradle my face I wanted more, I wanted to have him completely wrapped around me. I felt safe, cared for, seen. To have lived my life in a big house, yet all but invisible to the owners, being seen by this rough giant feels amazing.

I stand there, silently willing the hour to speed up so I can see him again. Gradually, the feel of the bag on my shoulder sinks into my consciousness and I know I have to change before his return. My face flames red again at remembering the younger guy's comment. Twice today, random guys felt the need to point out my unexpected period. Digging through the bag I find a pair of, thankfully black, yoga pants that I can easily wear with the t-shirt I have on.

Changing, and returning to the office, I have nothing to do but wait.

Sitting at the desk, I wrestle with the feelings I've had since laying eyes on Gunner less than an hour ago. Lightning bolt, *at first sight* type of feelings that can't possibly exist in the real world. I have absolutely no experience with boys. Well, he's not a boy. At all. He's got to be at least thirty?

How can I possibly express interest in him in a way that he'll take me seriously? Did he even feel anything close to what I did when he touched me? Slapping the desk, I just get more frustrated remembering why I'm here in the first place. I'm jailbait. He won't come near me.

Before long, I hear a motorcycle approaching. The louder the roar becomes the more excited I get. Yes, seventeen-year-olds get panty-soaking excited whether or not adults want to acknowledge it. Hearing the bike cut out then footsteps approaching I start to stand, only to get my shoelace caught in the wheel of the chair as I push it backwards.

Making my day complete, I fall in a graceless heap between the chair and the desk just as he enters. I'm once again on the ground staring up at Gunner, though more embarrassed than last time.

"We gotta stop meeting like this, Sweetheart," he's grinning down at me and extending his hand. "You ok?"

After pulling my shoelace out of the wheel, I take his hand to stand. "I'm a little off kilter today, to be honest," I reply with a self-deprecating grin.

"I'm gonna ask you some questions and I need you to be honest with me." Gunner turns, sitting in one of the chairs on the other side of the desk. Reaching into his vest he pulls out cigarettes and quickly lights one. He rolls his eyes in annoyance after I crinkle my nose at the smell.

Exhaling, he sits there with narrowed eyes that are fixed on me.

"How long until you're eighteen?"

"Eight and a half months. January 31." I reply as I try to figure out where this is going. I see some emotion flash across his face before he closes his eyes and exhales a cloud of smoke.

"And you live here, in town?" I nod, still trying to figure out his intent.

"Yes, I go to the university in..."

"I know where it is," he cuts in. "What are you studying?"

"Well...I'm in one program now, but I'm going to switch next year."

"Isn't that called Undecided, or some shit like that?"

"Typically. But in my case, it's more like my parents told

me what I would be studying and since I'm a minor..." There's that damn word again! I think we both cringe over it as I keep babbling. "Even though I'm a high school graduate I can't get emancipated, so I'm going to change majors next year. I've talked to a professor and if I keep my grades up I can probably get a partial scholarship and I've been saving up my allowance for living expenses."

"What degrees are we talking about here?" Gunner clearly can't imagine there being an issue.

"From pre-med to cyber security."

He laughs, "You want to be a hacker?!"

Without waiting for a reply, he shrugs and continues, "I'm thirty-two, I have a custom furniture business and do general woodwork on builds in this area. Then there are the Grizzlies, I'm the Sergeant at Arms," He tilts his head at me, as if trying to guess how much I've heard about the MC that basically runs this town. A lot actually, but I won't bring that up now.

"None of that is worth losing over..." he takes a deep drag on his cigarette as he continues to monitor me for a reaction. "Jailbait."

"Enough!" The word explodes out of me louder and more forcefully than I expected. Walking around the desk, I continue, "I didn't ask you for anything! I haven't done anything to you! I..."

"Haven't you, Sweetheart?" Gunner's deceptively low voice increases the tension in the room.

I look at him, beyond frustrated with his comment and at having nearly resorted to a rant myself. As I turn to grab my bags and leave the room, he reaches out, yanking me off my feet and dropping me onto the desk.

"Stay," he commands, leaving me in a sitting position on

the edge of the desk as he grounds out his discarded cigarette and retakes his seat.

Startled and flustered, I obey. Panting at the surprise turn this encounter has taken. Completely out of my element, I sit and wait for him to continue. He closes his eyes to stop their progression along my body and scoots his chair backwards.

"I won't touch you again," he starts, "not until February 1."

My mouth drops open and my eyes shoot to his.

"I want your number but that's not all," he continues and I am utterly incapable of anything but sitting still and waiting for his next statement.

Pausing to light another cigarette, he continues. "No dating anyone. If you're with someone now, you fucking end it today."

"I'm, I'm not. I, I've never been with anyone," I stutter in reply to his silence. My statement causes him to curl his hands into fists and growl. I mean actually growl.

Leaning forward in his chair, he is fighting his pledge not to touch me again. I can see that in his eyes and I revel in it. Exhaling, he slides his chair further back towards the door as the smoke curls over his head.

"There will be no contact between us, unless you need anything. If anything happens—another incident like today, which I will be looking into and I will make it stop—you reach out to me," Gunner commands and I know he means it. I also know I should be freaked out and running away right now. But cigarettes and all, I'd be much happier curled into his lap.

"Give me your phone," he holds out his hand to me and I almost reach for it. Stopping myself when he curls his fingers into a fist, I shake my head to clear it and reach into my bag for my phone. Taking it, he dials his own phone from it.

"Save the number," he says, handing it back.

I quickly do so while trying to absorb what he has said and watching him as he awaits my reaction. I know I have to assert myself. I want him, I'm too young for him right now but I refuse to sit meekly at home while he's out fucking his way through the state. "What happens February 1?"

"Well, that'll be a discussion for adults to explore, Sweetheart," he finally replies, drawing out the word 'explore' in a way that leaves no doubt what he wants to explore.

Squeezing my legs together draws his eyes towards the exact area of my body that has been throbbing since his return. That tempo is increasing by the moment and from the smirk on his face, he knows it too.

"This has to go both ways," I mumble. Not sure how to tell this man what I expect of him.

"What's that, Sweetheart?" He looks back up at my face, raising an eyebrow.

Studying my red Converses for all I'm worth, I finally form the words, "You want me to wait for you? Not to be with anyone else? I will, but only if you will."

Silence. But the silence isn't empty, it is very full. I know he's staring at me and I'll have to look up eventually and I'm gradually starting to feel pleased he isn't laughing, nor did he walk out. That has to be good, right?

"Come again?" Gunner asks very quietly.

OK, come on! It's less than a year! Miffed, I scoot off the desk and square my shoulders. This guy wants to punch my V card? He can flipping earn it.

"I'm not a complete idiot. I've heard there are girls that, you know, do whatever for the MC. And whoever else you come across. You asked something of me, I want the same from you!" My voice gets louder as I go on. The office door is open and I'm hoping that no one is in the waiting area, as that would really top off this banner day.

"Just to be clear. You don't want any hands, mouth, tits, pussy, or ass in contact with my hands, mouth, or dick until after our next...discussion?" I know he is going for shock value but I cannot help the look on my now beet red face. Looking him in the eye, he knows damn well no one has ever spoken to me this way and wants to give me a chance to run or back down. To know who he is and what he would expect.

As I start to speak, he throws in, "Or for me to watch others go at it while getting myself off?"

GUNNER

Her blush explodes simultaneously on her chest, visible through her white V-neck T-shirt, her neck, and her cheeks. Her jaw slackens, making me recite *Jailbait* over and over again in my mind. I don't think she's made up her mind yet of whether to hit me or take off, but I had started grinning when her small hands had curled up tight by the time I got to tits. Little Riley does have a backbone, alright.

Riley's next move really surprises me. She sits down again, her back is still ramrod straight and she crosses her arms across her chest; which pushes her tits forward. "Yep, no one's anything on any of you. And the other, I mean, I guess people watch porn?"

Fuck. This girl blushes anymore and she'll be in the burn unit. But I love that she isn't backing down.

"I meant watching in the flesh, Sweetheart, not porn." She really needs to stop making that "O" shape with her mouth.

"I'd rather you didn't." So prim and proper, like we're discussing something mundane.

Waiting until Riley's eyes make their way back to mine, I know I'm going to agree to this. But, fuck! That's a long time, I haven't screwed anyone in a couple weeks as it is. I guess I went through it during my deployments to Afghanistan though.

"I give you my word."

A megawatt smile lights up her face like nothing I've ever seen. She bounces back off the desk and takes a step towards me but I hold up my hand to keep her back, sliding my chair backwards again. "Really?" She asks.

Standing, my chair gets pushed back through the door. I get that she doesn't know me yet, but that shit won't fly with me. "I give my word on something, I mean it. A hundred percent. Don't question me on that, got it?" Towering over her, she takes a step back. That little movement pisses me off but I have no right to pull her towards me. Where she belongs.

CHAPTER THREE

GUNNER

Riley nods but before she can continue, Connal's voice rings out. "Hey, the SUV is all cle... Why's the chair in the hall?" Connal rams the chair into me as he guides it back into his office, not giving two fucks that he's interrupting.

Eagerly looking to him, she asks, "Is it alright?! How much do I owe you?" Clapping her hands together in front of her chest, she looks like he just handed her a new vehicle.

"We got the spray paint off, you may want to schedule a car wash with a wax to shine it back up a bit, but no one who didn't see it will notice anything. I'd say, with labor it'll be..."

"I'll take care of it," I say, nodding to Connal so he knows not to discuss it further.

Riley still reaches back to her bag and starts digging, pulling her wallet out and giving me her little glare again, she says, "Please, I can pay for it. You helped enough bringing me here, I won't let you pay. Connal, how much?"

She repeats and starts pulling cash out of her wallet. Like serious cash.

"The Fuck?! Connal, did you leave the safe open back here?" I can't help but raise my voice, besides the fact of the money, who the hell would pull that out in front of strangers? "Goddammit, Riley put all that away. Now!"

The three of us take turns looking at each other. Connal and I trying to figure out what seventeen-year-old walks around with what must be a few grand. Riley verbalizes her concerned expression. "I didn't steal it!"

"What?" Oh, my comment about the safe. "I know...I know you didn't steal it. Is that your tuition money?" I ask, trying to figure her out.

"No, my allowance," she returns like it's the most obvious thing in the world. Riley can't help but notice the stunned expressions on our faces and realizes how she sounded. "I mean, it's for the quarter," she says in a quieter voice, trying to minimize it. Suddenly, I want her out of there and away from Connal.

Maddock. She's a goddamn Maddock.

The last name she withheld from our introduction is screaming in my brain. I know whose child she is and this is going to turn into a shit show if Probie gets wind of it. This girl, this almost woman, is nearly legendary around here. Rowansville has nearly twenty thousand full-time residents and a thousand stories about why Riley has been hidden away.

Following behind her, I know that every single story is wrong. Riley has only been hidden away because her parents are the two most shallow, self-centered, conniving, greedy assholes in the state. So what could a child possibly do to further their powerbase and why should someone of their supposed calibre go to a local school?

Her SUV was pulled to the front of the shop and was indeed graffiti free. Taking in her relieved but tight smile, I can tell she'll still picture that word every time she looks at this vehicle. I can't help that though. I motion her into the front, as I open the back door to toss her bags inside.

"You'll text me? Let me know you got home okay?" I check.

"Yes, Gunner. A deal's a deal, right?" She confirms that we're still on, as she sticks her arm through the open window to shake my hand. "Thank you for helping with this. It really means a lot to me."

And I know she means it. She's not like so many other women in my life who put it on thick to try and get something from me.

"Sweetheart," I don't know if this is going to wreck things. "I'm beginning to put together who your parents are and it's gonna be complicated." She quickly flushes again and tries to pull her hand back from my grasp. "Let me finish!" I bark.

Easing up on my hold, I change my grip, keeping our thumbs hooked but wrapping my fingers up around her wrist. "A deal's a deal. But I want you to know it has nothing to do with them, not in my mind. Not while I was driving around earlier trying to think of how to make something of this. Eight and a half months can be a long time, just remember this started when you were in a puddle at my feet at the car wash—not a few minutes back when I figured out that you're a Maddock. Understand?"

Her eyes widen when I say her last name, then her sweet little smile is back, "I understand."

I release her hand and she gives me a little nod before driving away. I stand, watching her go, then move for my bike. Gonna pay a visit to her gram.

Eileen Riley is one interesting lady.

My parents were a mess. My mother had me her senior year of high school and I grew up hearing about how I ruined her life. It wasn't that she got knocked up by a married cop over twice her age that ruined her life. In her mind it was me. He wouldn't leave his family for her nor acknowledge me. In fact, he managed to keep my existence a secret until I was seven. That's when mom dropped me off at his mother's house and told her she was done dealing with my shit.

Grandma took one look at me and knew two things. The first was that I was the spitting image of her son, the second was that I needed to be in a hospital. The cold I was on baby aspirin for was actually pneumonia. From that day, until her death during my deployment, she loved me exactly how a mother should love a child.

It was while I was hospitalized with pneumonia that G'ma and Mrs. Riley became close friends. They had grown up in the same area, but different social standings were more strictly adhered to back then and kept them apart. Mrs. R volunteered in the children's wing of the hospital and as my G'ma was self-employed as a baker, she would sit and read to me when Grandma couldn't be there or visit with her while I was sleeping.

My G'ma, not sure how she was going to pay my hospital bill when I was released, was in turns mortified and thankful to learn that "it had been anonymously taken care of." She also pegged the culprit. Mrs. R was the only one around with the means or interest to do so.

G'ma started sending Mrs. R weekly checks to pay the balance down. They were always returned. Then one Sunday, she dressed me up and we drove to the Riley spread. G'ma had a plan. If Mrs. R wouldn't take the money then she would bake for her. With all of her charity events and dinners, surely this would be a benefit. I spent the visit in a kitchen larger than our home, feasting on sandwiches and hot chocolate while G'ma and Mrs. R discussed the "hospital matter" in the parlor.

Mrs. R, realizing she had wounded grandma's pride said she would consider her plan but somehow at the end of the hour had convinced G'ma that she would be doing her such a favor to set up shop in an abandoned storefront she owned, which coincidentally had an empty two-bedroom apartment over it. I never knew the details, but G'ma's bakery is still there. My half-sister runs it now.

Once I returned from my time in the Marines and made my way back here, I was met at G'ma's tombstone one day by Mrs. R's driver. Rogers handed me a note and after sizing me up warned me not to disappoint her.

In the most elegant of notes, I was invited to continue my G'ma's monthly visits to Mrs. R's, "but please note, I've decided to downsize and live in town now" was written in perfect penmanship. I was there the following Tuesday promptly at two, and every month since.

Today would be a surprise visit. Mrs. R had always done right by me. I owed her the respect of declaring my intentions.

CHAPTER FOUR

RILEY

JANUARY 25, 2018

I THOUGHT THE HOLIDAY SEASON WOULD NEVER END. Between houseguests from Boise and D.C. that my parents invited to the ranch and a forced week in Boise to be paraded in front of their political and business connections, I was a mess.

The good news about the hectic pace they set, my parents hadn't noticed my class schedule for this semester. *Operation Major Change* was successfully underway. Classes had started back a week ago and I was thrilled with them. When I could focus.

Bursting with nerves and with no one else to confide in, on New Year's Day and after swearing her to secrecy, I told my gram that I had changed my major. She gave me a huge wink and said, "Oh, is that all? Well, this will be such an exciting year for you, won't it, dear?" Then proceeded to giggle to herself. I've been watching her for further signs of dementia ever since.

I've kept to my deal with Gunner, although I make more frequent stops in town hoping to catch a glimpse of him. My heart accelerates every time I hear a bike around town. But any time I do see him, I end up more frustrated at our lack of contact than excited about seeing him.

I've gotten three texts from him. An acknowledgement of the first one I sent him, then what must have been a drunk message sent at well past midnight one night in early Fall—"*Im keeping my promise to u*"—and the last one after he received the Christmas present I had ordered and mailed to him. A silver lighter with the Grizzlies' logo etched on the flat sides and an R on the narrow side below the flint. "*Soon, Riley. Soon,*" was all that text contained.

Classes end for me at one today and with the money my parents gave me in lieu of a physical Christmas present, I am going to a salon near campus today. I'm getting a massage, facial, and then waxed *everywhere* below my waist. I have no idea what to expect next week but dammit, enough waiting for my life to start.

The one part about next week that made me the most nervous resolved itself this morning. Mother was working on paperwork at home and remembered to inform me that she and father were heading to Switzerland from the middle of January through the end of February. Happy Birthday to Me.

GUNNER - JANUARY 27

Fucking have to get to the clubhouse for Church. There's no missing that. This weather has been shitty and I've been working like hell to build up inventory. I want to really build up my furniture business and to get in with any of the stores in the area or to open my own, I have to have inventory. They won't take one piece with a promise of more down the line and for the first time in my life, I have to consider providing for someone other than myself.

Besides, throwing myself into the work is better than seeing my Brothers getting blown or screwing the club sluts. Been heading to Rusty's more and more so that shit isn't right in front of me. Flint and some of the others are there regularly, what with his Ol' Lady working there, he likes to keep close. The Girlies must have a bet going though, trying to wear me down. Never been hit with so much T&A as I have since I got back from SD last fall.

I've kept my word.

Granted I've also become a full-fledged stalker. I've been paying a security guard at the university to keep an eye on her and her SUV. A sister of one of the Ol' Ladies works in admissions there and gives me Riley's schedule each semester, so I'll know where she'll be. Friday nights she's with her gram.

And her gram, with that little fucking smile of hers. When I'm there every month. When I'm there talking about all things Not Riley, she'll occasionally throw out little lines like, "Oh, my granddaughter was by the other day and she..."

I've been going there once a month for seven fucking years and she may have mentioned her granddaughter twice, now she just throws out tidbits like confetti.

Last May, I went to Mrs. R and told her that I had met Riley and wanted her to be mine when she was eighteen like it was the 1800's and that was acceptable behavior.

She just smiled at me and said, "I'm so sorry I didn't think of that first. Do not screw it up." Then she changed the subject to something benign. But I could see the wheels turning in her head and have been waiting for all the scraps of information about Riley that she dangles in front of me. I crave them, but would never ask.

'Cause Riley's still fucking Jailbait for another four days.

Going through the motions at Church, I can barely focus on anything. Jasper, our President, notices but doesn't call me out. I have a feeling that's coming soon enough. Once we talk through upcoming deals and distribution options, Jasper opens the floor. Twenty fucking minutes spent on individual grievances like we're fucking kids and can't suck this shit up. Past that, Jasper asks the Officers to stay behind then adjourns the meeting.

Flint, Vice, Jas, and I are left. Jasper announces he and Emma are taking off for a week in March. Vice and Flint don't seem surprised so I imagine it's some of what I've missed the past couple weeks. He lays out what he needs from each of us during that time. Vice will be on distribution runs, so Flint will lead and I will still coordinate the other Enforcers while stepping up with local operations.

Looking at them and speaking up, "Brothers, I have something personal coming up. Club business is a priority, I understand, but ..." Shit, may as well go all in. "There's this girl..."

They all start laughing. "Yeah, no kidding. That why your dick's been dry a year?" Howls Vice.

"Shut. The. Fuck. Up." I growl. Flint and Jasper, having been there themselves, sit up a bit straighter. "She's not a goddamn hole. She's, well, she's more." I stand, pounding the table on the way up. Heading towards the door, I only pause and turn as Jas calls my name.

"Good luck. OK?"

"Yeah," I grunt back. "There might be some waves, but..." I shrug at Jas and Flint. "Yeah. See ya soon."

The party is in full swing in the main room. The Girlies seem occupied blowing or screwing various Brothers in the corners, while the Ol' Ladies are holding court near the bar. And I've gotta figure out how to bring a virgin into this. A virgin, whose father is Special Attorney assigned to Gang Activity by his best friend, the Governor of this state. A virgin, whose mother, an M.D., is classified as a Consultant to the Governor's Staff.

A sheltered virgin I've waited nearly a year for but will try to wait even longer for—until she's ready.

I am the worst kind of shithead. I know the whole situation is FUBAR, but am determined to make her mine. To own her. To claim her. My mother was tied down with me at that age and despised me, so to do that to this girl is the worst kind of fucked up. But I can't stop thinking of her eyes the first time I saw her and the primal need that came over me to take away her pain, to make her mine.

She sealed her fate when she stood up to me. Demanded something I would have nearly backhanded any other woman for suggesting. Demanding fidelity. She's had my fidelity these past eight-plus months and will have it, but it comes with a price. She's mine now. End of, or actually, beginning of story. And I will tear apart anyone who tries to take her from me.

Standing back against the bar, I barely register the beer in my hand or those around me. Feeling a tug on my cut, I look down ready to push away a Girlie or honey hole. But it's Bree.

"You ok, Handsome?" She yells up over all the noise.

"You take a night off Rusty's, Pretty Lady?" I duck her question, causing her to tilt her head to me in question.

"Real talk?" I query, knowing she'll keep what we say close to her vest. She's Flint's and well-liked, but still considered an outsider by most. She doesn't really talk about herself, and can be standoffish but has always been easy going with me.

"You know me Gunner, and you're one of the good ones, so let it out," she says and I nudge her away from the others to the corner of the bar. I unload. I had told Bree about my G'ma not long after she and I met, but I tell her everything about my monthly visits with Mrs. R and then later meeting Riley. I stop short of telling her my fears. That my wants and needs will push Riley away.

At one point, Flint had started to approach us, but Bree looked at him and shook her head. After looking back and forth between us, he nodded and sat across the bar. He wasn't drinking. He was talking to those around him but was just waiting, watching us. A man who had lived fast and hard but now in his mid-fifties, wanted nothing more than to go home with his new fiancé/Ol' Lady.

Flint is content to just let her be the woman that she is. I haven't known Bree long, but she sees things that others miss. She'll address them, fixing what she can and butting out when appropriate. Thinking about the two of them, I had stopped talking. She continued to sit quietly next to me, another trait I admire. When I glance towards her again, she finally gives me her two cents.

"Gunner, let me know when she'll be here. I know you don't have things figured out but trust me. This is a lot for an outsider. Speaking as one," she quickly adds, giving me a little half-smile. "Just text me, so I can try to buffer it. OK? I will make time for her, for you. Got it?"

Staring at my drink, I nod while standing. Turning to her I grab her, my unexpected bear hug causes her to laugh wholeheartedly. I see Flint rise and walk towards us. I set her back away from me but remind her, "Real talk, right, Pretty Lady? Just us for now?"

"I can't wait to meet her. Just between us." Then she turns and launches herself at Flint as he nears. "Take me home? I'm a bit horny," Bree mock-whispers in his ear.

"Gunner got you horny and you want to work it off with me?" Flint gruffly demands while she sucks in his earlobe. He's trying to hold his patented glare but throws a wink in my direction to let me know he isn't pissed. Guess he wants her to get creative when she makes it up to him.

"Flint, you sitting across from us tonight? All pissy? Reminded me of how you'd glare at me when I wouldn't go out with you?!" Bree leans back up to his earlobe. "Remember how that worked out?" She coos.

Without another word, Flint squats and tosses her over his shoulder and heads for the door – Bree's laughter is drowned out by the hoots and suggestions from all they pass.

CHAPTER FIVE

RILEY

JANUARY 31

I'M EIGHTEEN TODAY. I HAD AN EARLY DINNER WITH MY GRAM last night and I could barely sit still. My mind going a hundred miles an hour and my body humming, thinking of Gunner and trying to pay attention to the conversation at hand.

I cannot believe the gift she gave me! Well, I have to run by her place today to sign and date the contract, but she's gifting me a small building close to the shopping district. Gram owns several buildings in this town and the next one over; mostly storefronts with apartments above them. As of tomorrow, I will have access to a two bedroom apartment! I can move out of my parents' house!

The "you're an adult and I expect you to be responsible now" part came in next. I have to find and vet a small business to move into the empty storefront. Gram let me know the average rent prices for that area, but from that I have to pay property taxes and maintain the property. I know she'll guide me and even though I have no idea what I'm doing. I am so excited to have the opportunity to try.

But more than anything, today I can reach out to Gunner. I know he had said he would next see me on February first but I refuse to wait one more day to see him or touch him. Besides, he must have thought I would have plans with my parents today, right? They are a continent away, so rather than sit around and wait for what I want, I'm going after it.

After showering and trying on thirty combinations of jeans and t-shirts, I end up in the first set I tried on, a simple black V-neck tee and skinny jeans. Not wanting to look like I'm trying too hard, I forgo knee-high boots for my old standby—my red Converse Chuck Taylors.

I'm too anxious to eat, but don't know what is going to happen today so I scramble up some eggs with cheddar. Leaving shortly before nine, I head to grams and sign my first legal document.

"Well, here is your copy, Dear," she says handing me a set. "Now let's go and check over the space and then let's get some coffee and croissants.

"What?" I squeak. I have someplace I want to be.

"Dear, surely you want to see your new property?" Gram looks expectantly at me as I'm standing in her foyer ready to run. "You don't have plans I'm keeping you from, what with Ann and Bill out of the country?"

I feel like a deer in headlights, but also like she's mocking me. Standing there with my jaw open, I know I have to agree to her unexpected plans but there's this glint in her eyes. I quickly agree to her proposed outing. There's no way to really explain I am about to run out and throw myself at a thirty-something biker. There's no way that anyone who has ever met me would think that.

The next two hours of my life are torture. The building is adorable, some parking in back, a nice area for the business I need to recruit, and a newly renovated two bedroom apartment. I cannot believe every detail gram thought of for me and feel miserable that I want to run off. Gram starts talking about items like getting the electric, gas, water, and garbage services all transferred to me and that's when it really occurs to me to get my head out of the clouds and pay attention. Suddenly, having a million questions to ask about these things, I shake off what I want to do and get down to business with gram. Day one of adulting, I guess.

Dropping gram off at the salon, and shaking nearly as hard as the day I met Gunner, I head out to the Grizzlies' clubhouse. Pulling into the lot, I take a deep breath and get out of my SUV. There are a few guys hanging around outside, two with leather vests like Gunner had on when we met. They're smoking and stop to watch me approach. I have to get around them to get inside.

The heaviest of the three immediately makes a suggestion, which will just never happen. The guy without the vest tells me he doesn't mind sloppy seconds, which he's calling unless I want to start with a DP. Before I can gather myself to say anything, the third guy, who is tall and slim, tells me to get lost.

"No." I am beet red and seriously rethinking my surprise visit, but also see Gunner's bike parked off to the side. That spurs me on.

Tall, scary guy steps towards me, "No? The fuck you say, this is my house, Princess, you don't belong."

"No. Gunner. I'm here for Gunner." Becoming more angry than scared, I seriously question my sanity.

He laughs and turns back to the others, who are still blocking my way inside. I step towards them when the sound of more bikes coming into the lot makes me turn.

Yes! I have an in. There are five of them, but in the middle of the pack, I spot Connal riding without a helmet.

I stay where I am as they secure their bikes, then just as I'm about to call out to Connal, the tall guy grabs my shoulder pushing me back towards my SUV.

"Get the fuck outta here, Princess, or you won't like what happens next," he growls. Meanwhile, the heavy guy strokes his penis and starts talking about running a train on me.

"Connal," I yell out, not that we haven't garnered everyone's attention already. "Connal, can you let Gunner know I'm here."

Even Connal is staring at me like I'm nuts. "Jailbait? You're Jailbait, right?" He asks, getting everyone laughing.

"Not anymore." I grimace at the reminder.

"Well then, come on in, sugar, and let's see what Gunner's gonna give you for your birthday," he says smirking at me, the other men go into overdrive making comments and volunteering shoulders to cry on.

I've come this far, why not follow him into the Grizzlies' den?

CHAPTER SIX

GUNNER

Why the fuck did I tell her tomorrow? Today's her birthday, so she has to be with her parents, right? I want to get to her now, not tomorrow dammit.

I'm craving a smoke and on my second whiskey although it's barely noon. Sitting at the bar, I can hear a few of the other guys are further back in the room getting their wood attended to by whichever women are still around from the night before, while Roy shows our newest probie the ropes behind the bar.

From the yelling and laughing, it sounds like the party has kicked off in the parking lot. Shooting back my drink, I look over to the door as it opens, and promptly spit it back out.

Standing in the doorway framed by light is Riley. Fuck. Not here, not like this. Connal quickly steps up behind her, giving her a little shove while her eyes adjust to the dim light in here. Following her line of sight, I nearly shit myself as the first thing she sees is Needle spraying his cum on a Girlie's face in the back of the room. Goddamn fucking hell!

I'm up and calling her name, getting her to focus on me while Connal is still pushing her further in, followed by Brothers who want front row to what they hope will be a show. Her eyes are wide and startled by the sight that greeted her. She quickly looks behind me and seems to exhale when she can see I was sitting by myself. I've gotta keep her calm. Shit.

I reach her, cupping my hands on either side of her face. "Today's my birthday," she whispers. "I thought waiting another day was..."

Leaning down to her ear, "Sweetheart, I was just thinking the same thing. Come with me, ok?" At her nod, I start to lead her back towards my room but Frank reaches up from behind Connal and makes the mistake of grabbing her arm.

"Where ya going, Gunner? Don't be shy, we'd all like to see her get it." He cackles as Riley grabs me around my waist with her free arm.

"Gunner?" She softly cries out.

"That's right Honey, we all share around h..." My right fist cuts up to his jaw, ending the scene for now, though there'll be hell to pay later. I reach down and with an arm behind Riley's knees and shoulders, pick her up, quickly walking towards my room in the back while ignoring the comments and glares from Brothers and a Girlie or two. She has snuggled into my chest and is shaking. Fuck. How do I make this right with her?

Shifting her slightly to get my keys out of my pocket, her shaking has increased and she lets out a little noise that sounds like, like a...giggle? Locking the door behind me, I peer down at her and she is laughing almost silently into my chest. What is wrong with her?

"Sweetheart?" I start, then stop, putting her down and starting to smile with her, although I'm not sure why.

"I wanted to surprise you," Riley gasps out. "I guess that backfired."

"No, I am pretty surprised," I respond, running my hand through my hair. "I had a little different plan for how I wanted this to go..."

"Did it involve a guy suggesting I run a train in the parking lot or seeing another guy shoot cum in a woman's face? Otherwise, I think I win." She giggles again. How is she laughing, why isn't she running?

Sitting down on the end of my bed and pulling her in between my legs, all I can do is take this second chance she's handing me. "Happy Birthday, Sweetheart," I say, wrapping my hand up around the back of her neck and, finally, pulling her mouth to mine.

RILEY

I'm dreaming. It's really the only explanation. Gunner's hand is tangled in my hair, against the back of my neck and he has just taken control of me. His lips go from gentle to possessive and I melt into him.

His tongue is gently pressing against my lips and I quickly give him access to my mouth. I don't want this kiss to ever end. His other hand slides my jacket down before wrapping around my body, pulling me further into him. I curl my arms around his neck but I get so eager that my teeth bump against his, jolting me a bit. Mortified, I lean back against his arms that are keeping me close to him, ending our kiss.

"Sorry," I mumble, moving my face to lightly kiss his check. His hand, still secured on my neck, pulls my head back.

"Open your eyes, Sweetheart." His voice is raspy and unfamiliar now. As I slowly comply, he holds me still so I'm staring into his eyes. "I'm gonna teach you everything, okay? No saying 'sorry', never with me. You got that?"

My heart, which had started to slow, immediately speeds back up to hummingbird pace. "I, I don't know what to do, I mean, exactly." I stammer, trying to maintain eye contact.

"Well, for starters, how do you feel about lunch?" He suggests, grinning at me.

My jaw drops open and all I can think is how badly I've screwed today up. I don't belong here and I don't know how to kiss so now I'm getting the first step of a brush off. Squaring my shoulders and putting my hands on his biceps, attempting to escape his hold and lean down for my jacket, I look towards the door trying not to cry. "I should go...sorry to... well, come here unannounced." I twist away.

I'm reaching for the doorknob when he places his arms on either side of me, holding the door closed. He leans down, whispering in my right ear, "We are not done, Sweetheart. Where you running to?"

"You don't want...I shouldn't have come, um, I mean..." I stop stammering, staring straight ahead at the door while planning the path to my car past the bikers and women in the front room.

"Shhhhh," he hums in my ear. "I want you. I kept my promise to you. I love that you were ballsy enough to come here and didn't back down. I want you, for far longer than today so we're going to lunch. I'm not fucking you today. I've never attempted a relationship before and I've waited this long, so just stick with me through the gauntlet out there, okay Sweetheart?" He soothes me, before turning me and lifting my chin to look back into his eyes, waiting for my agreement. I know he won't accept anything less.

"My SUV is out front," I'm just stating the obvious here. "Should I drive?"

"Ha. I almost forgot!" He grins, looking all excited and turning back to his bed. Reaching underneath, he pulls out a carefully wrapped box. "Your present!"

"Really?!"

Holding it just beyond my reach and grinning madly, he says, "So grabby! Let me tell you something first." I pause in my attempt to reach my prize. Still holding the box away from me, he reaches down, holding the back of my neck again. "I've never had a woman on the back of my bike before."

I tear into the present as soon as he releases it. It's a helmet. I look from it to him. "You don't take women for rides?"

"No Sweetheart, you'll be my first." He wiggles his eyebrows making me laugh as I try on the helmet and turn to the mirror over his dresser. "We can look into some decals or something for it or just collect them as we go on rides, I didn't know what you'd like."

Leaning back into him and drawing his arms around me as we study each other in the mirror, I know I am unreasonably excited about the helmet. All I can think is that this larger than life man, with beautiful eyes and an amazing smile, wants me with him. Wants to keep me safe and by his side.

He rests his chin on the top of the helmet and maintaining eye contact, he slowly slides his hands from where I'm holding them crossed in front of my midsection. Moving them upwards, while waiting and watching for my reaction, he cups my breasts. Overwhelmed and wanting more, I arch into his palms. He responds by shifting his fingers over my nipples, which have turned into diamond hard points.

"Perfect handfuls, Sweetheart," he grins down at me through the mirror, tightening each of his large hands.

Moaning, I close my eyes as I let him draw me tighter into his chest. My eyes startle open again as he slides his right hand in through the top of my v-neck tee and rolls my left nipple between his thumb and finger. I know for a fact that I've never been as wet between my legs as I am right now. His eyes have become hooded, dark with something I've never seen before.

"Keep your eyes on me, Sweetheart. I need to see what you like." My hands stretch up to remove the helmet, desperate to be able to kiss him again. When his left fingers start simultaneously rolling my right nipple through the fabric of my shirt and bra, my knees buckle.

"Please," I beg without knowing exactly what I need. Turning me, Gunner lifts and places me on the dresser. Just as quickly, he has lifted the front of my shirt over my head but leaves it halfway off to secure my arms. Mewling and trying to free myself, he grabs my shoulders, lightly shaking me.

"Leave it," he growls. Stretching his thumbs back over my breasts he snags the lace cups of my bra down over my erect nipples, pushing my breasts together he leans down, swirling his tongue between each hardened point.

I seem to be moaning "Please" on repeat, I can't hold a thought. I just want this feeling to last forever. Needing more, I tilt my hips forward wrapping my legs around his waist and grinding myself against his...holy shit! I've never felt a cock before but the ones I've seen in Anatomy class were not, I mean, his feels so long and thick. As he continues to alternately tweak or suck my nipples, I accelerate my movements up and down the bulge I feel through our jeans. The seam of my jeans helps to stimulate my clit and within moments I shatter, screaming his name.

During my frenzy, one of his arms had moved around my waist to secure me to him while the other holds my face as he scatters kisses all around as he murmurs, "Let go. Give it to me, Riley."

Sagging against him, he deftly readjusts my bra and shirt. "That's my Sweetheart, coming so hard for her man." I moan in embarrassment and slap my hands against either side of my face, thinking to hide myself from his knowing eyes, I push deeper into his chest.

"Sorry!"

Cupping my face again and moving me away from the comfort his chest provides, he repeats himself. "This is your last free warning, Sweetheart. No saying 'sorry' to me. Tell me you understand you're getting punished next time."

I nod until his glare tells me he expects more. "I understand."

"Good, now how about that lunch?" He smirks down at me.

GUNNER

Stepping back from her, I can see she caught my double meaning and isn't sure what I'm offering for lunch. Her eyes are wide and staring at the outline of my rock hard cock straining at my jeans.

"You know you have the most perfect tits I've ever seen." I love it when she blushes, so I adjust my cock to see what she'll do next. I didn't expect Riley to lose it just now and dry hump my dick, good to know I can get her all worked up by sucking on her tits. I'll be taking real good care of those in the future.

Reaching down to pick up her helmet and jacket, I toss them to her saying, "Food, Sweetheart, I don't mean to disappoint you but I'm talking about food."

"What about you?" She challenges, flashing her amber eyes up to mine.

"Baby steps, Sweetheart." Pinning her up against the door again and dropping a kiss on her forehead, "We'll talk over lunch, there's some things we gotta sort out before I claim you."

"Claim me?" Riley repeats. "Bit of a caveman, aren't you?"

"You have no idea. But now, we're going out to my bike and you gotta do what I say." She grimaces, thinking about the reception we'll receive, but nods. "Hold my left hand and stay real close. If Frank thinks to start anything, I'll need my right hand free. If Jas or Flint are out there, they may want to talk to me before we go. That happens, I'm bringing you back here until I can get away. Got it?"

Riley leans up and shyly kisses my chin. "I'm stronger than you think, Gunner."

Placing my forehead against hers, "I don't doubt that, but they got to get used to seeing you and know they can't touch you. They're all a few drinks in now, so stay close to me."

"Only place I want to be," she says firmly, reaching for my hand while gripping her helmet in her left hand.

We're nearly halfway across the room before Hawk yells out to me, trying to wave me over. I shake my head at him and try to get through the group, most of who are now trying for a peek at Riley. Connal and Royce, who was a probie the last time he was near Riley at the garage, fall in behind me.

"Keep going," Connal says, "Last I saw Frank and his buddies, they were heading back outside. Just watching your back, Brother."

"His back? Why watch his when hers is so fucking tight?" Royce still hasn't learned to keep his trap shut. Unable to decide between turning on him and getting Riley outside without incident, I look over my shoulder when I hear him grunt and Riley says, "Oops, sorry!" In an overly cheerful voice, she just gives me a very satisfied looking smile and shrugs. Guess she's making use of that helmet right away.

Ignoring comments from those we pass, mainly about cherries and fresh meat, we get outside and I immediately see my guard was not needed. A few groups of people had spilled outside, but not seeing Frank, Flint, nor Jas anywhere around, I know I can at least get outta here with my girl and answer for the sucker punch later.

"Connal, Royce, appreciate it," I throw over my shoulder.

"Isn't he Probie?" Questions Riley, who seems to want to stand and chat now.

"I got Patched, Honey. Too bad you missed the party, you'd have enjoyed it!" He winks at her. Yeah, he gave facials to most of the Girlies and then made a sandwich out of a few honey holes who wandered in for the party. I'm sure Riley would have loved that.

Connal laughs but pulls back on Royce's arm, "Have fun but be sure to wrap that shit up, Gunner! No matter how hot Jailbait here is, you're too fucking ugly to spawn." And these are my Brothers.

Turning to Riley, I help her with her helmet and tell her what not to do sitting on the back of my Hog. Getting on first, and then pulling her snug against me after she mounts up, I decide on the next town over for lunch. Eager for time away from familiar faces and the opportunity to talk somewhere I won't have a bed nearby to bury myself in her, we head off down the road.

Interesting experience for me. At first, she's plastered to my back, trying to squeeze the breath out of me. Right as I slow to make sure she's alright, she gradually eases back. Keeping her right hand secured on my belt, she slides her left around to my back and seems to take a look around. Next, she is curled back up to me, but her hands are set apart and not trying to span my waist. Her chest is no longer smashed up against me, but loosely pressing into my back. I laugh to myself, thinking this is how our relationship will be. First, she'll be worried maybe insecure, then more comfortable and come out of her shell. But I know that the last part when she's just happy being curled into me will be the best feeling of all.

Pulling into an overpriced but decent brewpub some hipsters opened a year ago, I usher Riley in and indicate a booth in a relatively quiet corner. Not waiting on the host who scurries behind us, I cut him off not interested in his speal. Not interested in anything but making Riley mine.

"You enjoy that ride, Sweetheart?"

"Almost as much as the earlier ride!" She quips back, lightly blushing and laughing at herself. "I was scared at first but then it just felt so good! Thank you for my helmet!"

"Don't got to thank me. Keeping you safe is on me from now on. Waiter's coming, let's get our order in then we talk."

Cutting the kid off before he can launch into specials, we quickly place our orders. A diet coke for her and the house lager for me.

While I'm trying to figure out what to start with, Riley speaks up. "I should have texted you earlier, my parents are out of the country and I saw my gram this morning but

I don't have anything else going on till classes on Monday."

Groaning, knowing that she's home alone makes my cock start to twitch again. Waiting until our drinks are dropped off, I start in.

"So your parents, let's start there. That's going to be an issue with my Brothers. I need to know more about your relationship with them. How dependent are you? I know you're in school, do they control you with that? Anything else I should know?"

She starts talking and I'm more relieved and impressed by the moment. In changing her major under her parents' nose, she was able to secure a scholarship. This also means she'll be done in two years rather than five, then she explains how in demand this degree is with many home-based positions available, just needing a secure, high-speed network. I can make that work. I mean, she started university at sixteen so I knew she was smart, but listening to her is another story.

She goes on to confirm what I know from her gram, that she basically has no relationship with her parents. They parade her around their associates when necessary to maintain appearances and are financially generous with her but otherwise absent from her life. She gives me a pointed look when she talks about their careers.

It's their relationship with the Governor and the fact of who I am and what I do, that will set her father on me and my Brothers' like never before.

"What do you know about the MC?" I continue, as she pauses to dig into her sandwich that had just arrived.

"You mean other than your charity rides and community service days?" She smirks at me, licking mustard off her finger.

"Yeah, smart ass, other than that." I laugh, while focused on the finger she had licked.

"Ahh, is that what you were doing earlier?" She asks me. I frown as I have no idea what she's talking about, so she continues. "You were checking me for a wire, weren't you?" She says, grinning hugely at me.

Chuckling, and finishing the last of my beer as the waiter deposits a fresh one, "Why don't you slide over to this side and I'll continue checking while we talk?"

"Nope, I won't be able to form sentences," Riley replies playfully, getting a growl from me. "Ok, so from what I've heard you guys run guns and drugs. I think a past leader cut the, um, prostitutes?"

"Past President, yep, no women. But if we're together, you can't do any talking about anything else you overhear. You give me your word on that cause it will be my life otherwise. I have to be able to trust you." I stare her down, so she'll know how serious this is.

"That's just it, isn't it?" She queries, meeting my stare. "I have to trust you're with me for me, not to get at my family. If I'm with you, I, well, I don't have a relationship with my parents anyway but my gram is important to me. I think she might come around eventually, but I have to be able to trust you aren't using me."

"About that..." I pause, not sure how she'll take this next part.

"About what?" She pushes looking anxious.

"Your gram. I've already talked to Mrs. R." Silence.

She seems to swallow every sentence she tries to start, so I continue. "I've known her since I was a kid, she and my grandmother were friends. I never knew anything about you. She'd mention her granddaughter from time to time but I guess I always pictured a child. That day we met, after I figured out who you were and you drove away, I went to her. I told her I wanted you."

Stopping for a breath and to shake my head at the waiter as he tries to approach, I ignore the frown forming on Riley's face and continue. "She sat in her parlor and listened as I convinced her that I would be good for you, then I talked myself out of it. I mean, your parents, right? Then I kept talking about the pain I saw in you, about your sweetness and your laugh. She got tired of my pacing at some point and demanded I sit down."

Smiling over at the perplexed expression on Riley's face, "She said that you were the most precious thing in the world to her and, while I certainly couldn't screw up any more than your parents had, that she would shoot me herself if I hurt you and I had better be done whoring around because that was no longer acceptable."

Riley sits quietly processing all I've said. Finally, she leans towards me, trying to suppress a smile. "I can't believe her! You know she tortured me all morning?! I had to swing by her place to sign something and she kept me for two hours, with a 'why, Dear, you don't have any plans today, do you?' in her sweet gram voice. Argh! I can't believe she knew all along!"

Reaching across and moving her mostly ignored plate aside, I take her tiny, soft hands in mine. "I go see her once a month and since that day I told her I wanted you I never brought you up again, didn't want to push my luck. She would volunteer information or cute little stories from time to time to string me along.

"Once she said she should have taken you into her home when you were young but that she thought with you there, your parents would come around. That they'd see there is more to life than power and money."

Looking at Riley's eyes swell with tears is too much for me, I move around to her side of the booth to pull her into my arms. Pressed up against my chest, she tells me about how she asked her gram for that once, and what her mother did to her afterwards. She passes it off as an accident but that does nothing to cool my anger at a child being abused, then locked in her room overnight with an untreated broken collarbone. I am more resolved than ever to make her mine, to love her like she's never been loved before.

The word love echoes in my mind. I push her back from my chest to search her eyes again. Can she teach me how to love? To trust? I know I want her like I've never wanted anything, but love? Fuck.

A hand touches my shoulder and I nearly strike without thinking, pushing Riley against the wall, I stop just short of hitting the waiter. He stutters something about a shift change, throws the bill on the table and hightails it back to the kitchen. I now notice that in between the lunch and dinner shift, the restaurant is nearly deserted so I throw some bills down as Riley excuses herself for the bathroom.

Meeting her near the entrance, I noticed the weather has taken a turn from the sun and clear skies that made for nice riding earlier. Going back will be slower.

"Where to, Gunner?" Riley asks, sliding her arm around my waist.

"Come to my shop," I say without thinking.

"You have a store?" She asks in surprise.

"Not yet, I have a workspace where I build custom furniture but I'm working towards getting a store. Flint, he's kinda the Chairman now, his kid built a website for me and taught me a bit about social media, so orders come in through there or from locals or people who vacation here." She has raised her eyebrows and is smirking at me as she secures her helmet. "Yeah, I'm not really social media savvy yet," I admit.

"But you want a store?" She pushes. I nod, getting on the bike.

"That's a little way off, I think." Pulling back on the road home, Riley is initially nervous again but quickly relaxes and snuggles into my back.

The next twenty minutes are bliss. The cold air hitting me helps me clear my mind and keeps my wood in check. It wasn't until we're turning off onto the driveway that I realize she had left her gloves behind and I drag her inside to run her hands under warm water.

"Shit, Riley! Why didn't you signal to me?"

Between chattering teeth, "I guess I left them in the booth, I just didn't think and then I didn't want to bother you on the way here." Pulling our jackets off, I quickly wipe her wet hands off on my shirt then stick them under it, up against my chest to warm them.

"Sweetheart, we'll get you a good pair and keep them in the saddlebag, ok? Next time you need me to stop, tug twice on my jacket and I'll pull off as soon as it's safe." I hold her as her shivers ease and she leans back.

"I'm sor..." My mouth descends roughly on hers before she can apologize.

"What did I tell you about saying 'sorry'?" I ask, pulling myself away from her sweet mouth.

"How are you going to punish me?" She asks, rolling her eyes that are filled with laughter. Now is a good a time as any to show her what I like, so I spin her around and bend her over a console table I finished last week.

Ignoring her startled gasp, one hand firmly pushing on her back and the other rubbing circles on her ass, I say 'count' before drawing my right hand back and spanking her firmly. When nothing but a soft cry escapes her lips, I reach up to gather her hair in my left hand while gently rubbing the spot where I spanked her.

"I told you to count, Sweetheart. Don't make me start over," I whisper, getting a soft moan in response this time.

"One," she finally says. Taking this as permission, I continue, bringing her up to a five-count before pulling her lips up to my mouth while rubbing her ass and trying not to lose control and fuck her on the floor of my shop.

CHAPTER SEVEN

RILEY

At first, all I could think was that my ass is on fire, then that heat spread to the front and I know that I'm soaked. If this is what he wants of me, I'm in.

As Gunner tries to ease back from our kiss, I hold tighter behind his neck and brace myself as I slide first one leg then the other up around his hips. My legs secure around his waist, I've locked us together and he deepens the kiss, turning and pushing my back against a wall. Thrusting his cock against me, I drop my hands, trying to get his belt open to reach the prize beneath.

"No, no, no," he starts to chant into my mouth before breaking away. "Not now. There's no going back for you once we start. I won't let you go."

"Don't stop," I beg. I don't recognize who I am right now, and all I can feel is this burning need to be possessed by him. "Please don't stop."

"Sweetheart, look at me. Come on." He places feather

light kisses around my face and I concede, sliding my legs back to the floor but moving into his chest. Sighing against him, his next words rumble against me. “I need to know, I need you to tell me, did you like that?”

I swear I’ll forever be beet red around this man! “I did,” I whisper, shy again and look up at him to see him smile widely down at me. “That’s a thing with you? You’ll want to...do that, regularly?” I burst out, trying to figure out what I’m in for with him.

“Yeah, that’s one of my ‘things.’ I’m gonna go slow with you, but I’m not a gentle man.” He murmurs in his rough voice while kissing my forehead. “I won’t ever harm you though, you understand me, Riley?”

I reach up to soothe the crease that has formed between his brows and start to answer, until I register our surroundings. Wood furniture is neatly stacked or hung from hooks on the wall and the first pieces that catch my eye can only be described as art.

Diverted, I move around him to start playing with a coffee table that seems more like a puzzle box, it’s in a similar dark wood shade to the table where he spanked me and I’m in awe.

“Gunner! Will you sell me this table?” I squeal in excitement. I know how I’ll furnish my new apartment.

Looking up at him, he seems to have become the shy one now. “You like it, Sweetheart? Take what you like.”

“What? No! I want to buy it, oh – I need more furniture actually.” I hadn’t gotten around to telling him about the present from my gram. I wasn’t sure what to say, as I don’t want to come across as completely spoiled. “I’m moving into an apartment in town. I think I can take my bed from home, but I haven’t told my parents about it yet, so that might be weird. Right?”

"Slow down. What do you mean moving?" He pulls a chair from a hook on the wall, moving it close to me he sits and pulls me up onto his lap in one motion.

"It was kind of a surprise from gram. It's over on Beckett near Main? It has two bedrooms. I've got to figure out changing over the electric, gas, and everything tomorrow but I'll need furniture. I've been saving up my allowance forever anyway, so I will pay you. You've worked hard on this."

"Mrs. R just happened to give you your own place, did she? Right ahead of an expected blow up with your folks about your major? And me?"

"I had told her about changing my major and YOU had filled her in about us, you know, maybe dating, or whatever, so she had a bit of time to think it out, I guess," I reply, following the swirl of his tattoo up his wrist. He grips my hand, stopping the progression and trying to keep us on track this time. Standing to further explore his work, I tug on his hand to join me. "What about you, do you live here or at the clubhouse?" Silently praying it's the former.

"I have a couch, bathroom, and small kitchenette here but live at the club. Have since I Patched up, most of the single guys do. Bought this land about four years ago, this workshop was already here, this plus three acres."

I groan. I can't help it. I knew I was going to have to go back to the clubhouse to get my SUV, but to possibly sleep there with him? Ew.

Understanding what I'm thinking, he comes up with an easy, temporary solution. "My truck is out back, we'll switch to that then run by the clubhouse so I can grab a change of clothes and your SUV. I'll follow you into town and we'll stay at a hotel. You do want to stay with me tonight, Sweetheart?"

I love how he says ‘Sweetheart’, almost as much as the look he’s giving me, filled with promises. “Yes, I, um, just not there, not the clubhouse.” As he lifts my chin up with his finger, I notice the crease between his eyebrows has returned.

“You get a pass today, Riley, but those are my Brothers and that is my home. I haven’t touched the Girlies or anyone else since we made our deal, I can’t change the past and I will not apologize for it. It’s part of what comes with me.”

“What do you mean, exactly, when you say ‘Girlies’? And you mentioned Flint earlier, can you tell me more?” Gunner’s made references to both and I’m not entirely certain of any of it.

Moving to the back room with me wrapped around him like my weight is insignificant; he grabs two beers from a small fridge and motions me to the couch. “What’s your tolerance level like, Sweetheart?” He smirks, handing me a bottle.

“I’ve never had beer before!” I reply, sending him into a choking fit over Gunner’s first sip. “I’ve had wine with my family, then I went to a frat party last year and there was some kind of punch, not that it had any juice in it.”

“Jesus Christ, I forget how young you are!” He says before launching into a breakdown of the Club. Jasper, the current President and his wife, Emma; Flint and Bree, and so on until all the names are jumbled together. Then on to what I wanted to know.

“The Girlies, they’re affiliated with us but not like the Ol’ Ladies. They’re not with any one guy, not to say that sometimes they don’t become someone’s Ol’ Lady. We protect them, they party with us, most work in one of the businesses we run and a few take care of the cleaning and cooking at the clubhouse. They are also available to take care of any

Brother who has an itch to scratch. I think there are about eight or ten now. Then there are honey holes, women who come in to party but aren't affiliated with the Club."

"And an 'Ol' Lady' is a wife?" I'm still not sure of the title.

"Sometimes. When someone takes an Ol' Lady, they announce it to the group at a gathering then Flint, Jasper, or Vice have to approve it. That means you trust her to put the Club first, that she's yours alone and completely under your protection. That if she missteps, you'll take the heat for it. None of the other guys ever lay a finger on her, and faithfulness usually comes with it too. How can you trust a woman to protect you if she's pissed at you for sticking your cock other places? The Girlies usually stay clear 'cause the Ol' Ladies can get them cut off, so they don't want the aggravation." Taking a swig, he presses on.

"It's not a marriage though. Jasper and Emma did get married, Flint's engaged to Bree, but some of the guys, like Wrench, has been with his Ol' Lady a decade or so and they have three kids together but never married. Like anywhere else, I guess. You coming to the clubhouse today was tricky. Coming in like that is what girls do when they want to party, y'know? Get some action? You came alone, so you were considered open season for whomever."

"Shit." Now it's my turn at taking a swig of beer, once I realized how stupid my 'surprise' was. "What will happen with you and that guy?"

"Frank? He's an asshole anyway, but as Sergeant at Arms, I'll have to make it right. I can't go swinging at guys who don't see anything out of the ordinary about their actions." Gunner shrugs. "The Club is the closest, we'll go there first. Want to show me your new place next? We can measure areas to see what will fit?"

"You'll help me? I hadn't even thought of that." I admit,

feeling more and more my age. “And I am paying you for whatever furniture I pick, or I won’t take anything. Got it?”

He shrugs again then tells me to grab my coat while he digs out a measuring tape. Taking my time walking back through the shop, I really am impressed by the quality of the work. Slipping on my jacket, he quickly steps in to help guide my arm into the second sleeve, kissing my ear and reaching around the front to zipper me up. “Want me to warm the truck up before you come out, Sweetheart?”

Regardless of his scar, I really cannot believe this man is single. He’s so thoughtful. “No, I’ll be fine now. I’m just sad I can’t sit wrapped around you for this ride.”

He laughs at my admission, but I really mean it. With his bike secured, we head over to his Explorer then go back to the clubhouse. Once there, he parks near my SUV and tells me to sit tight. Halfway out the door, he turns back and grabbing me behind the neck pulls me in for another kiss, taking absolute possession of my mouth then releasing me before I can muster a thought.

“No running off with any bikers now, Sweetheart!” He laughs as he gets out. “You’re all mine.”

A few minutes after he disappears inside, a Silverado pulls into the lot. I’m not at the right angle to see much more than her auburn hair, most of which is under a large cowl scarf. I’d kill for that color hair. Mine is just plain brown. Although my mother mentioned me getting highlights to look more appealing, I’ve never actually done it. Looking back over her shoulder she catches a glimpse of me, then stares at the truck again. When she looks back to me, I give her a little wave not knowing what else to do.

That seems to have made up her mind and she heads over to the passenger side door. I open it on her approach and smiling she asks, “Are you with Gunner?”

Suddenly unsure of myself, and not wanting to put Gunner in another awkward position, I go with, "I'm waiting for him, yes. And I'm absolutely not pulling any trains."

She bursts out laughing uncontrollably and I know instantly we'll be friends. Looking at her from the seat of his truck, I can see that she's old enough to be my mother. Although her hair looks natural with her coloring, the lines around her eyes and mouth as she laughs give her away. "I'm Bree, are you Riley?"

I nod, surprised she knows my name and reach my hand out to shake her offered hand. I pictured someone closer to my age when Gunner spoke of her earlier and am suddenly intimidated by how confident she is.

"I'm going to kill Gunner. I told him to let me know when he'd bring you here, I wanted to, well Hell, watch out for you a bit. It can be a little crazy." She shrugs and I quickly nod my head in agreement.

"He wasn't expecting me today, but it's my birthday and I didn't want to wait until tomorrow."

"Happy Birthday then! Considering your talk of pulling trains, I'm sure you had an interesting welcome?!" Again nodding in reply, I'm now certain I'm going to like her. "Gunner's a quiet one," she continues, "but he had a few drinks the other night and told me about you. I kept it between us like he wanted, oh, here he comes. Quick program my number in your phone!"

She's reaching for it the moment I take it out. "Anytime you need to talk, any questions I can answer, ok?"

"What are you doing, Bree?" Gunner yells out when he's about ten feet from us. She slides my phone back to me.

"You appointed me the welcoming committee when you confided in me the other night, just holding up my end." She winks at me, "Flint'll be here soon, you may want to head out before you get dragged back inside. You be good to her, Gunner. Nice meeting you, Riley!"

Without waiting for any replies she heads towards the door to the clubhouse and I turn to Gunner. "I like her! Follow me to the apartment, ok?" Taking a page from Bree, I jump out and go to my car without waiting for his reply.

GUNNER

I had basically run through the front room of the club and shoved items at random into a duffle. Heading back through, I let Connal know to text me if I'm needed but that I won't be around otherwise. He smirks and makes a comment about me losing my virginity tonight. I walk away thinking, not tonight Brother.

After close to a year, the label feels about right but I don't want to rush this. It's not like fucking Christmas morning. That always sucked. Months of getting excited over the build-up then Wham! It's done. No, I'm going to fucking earn her cherry and then savor the hell outta it.

Stepping back into the cold, I see that the passenger side door of my truck is open. With the interior light on, I can see Riley smiling but, suddenly anxious, I move faster until I realize she's speaking to Bree. Thank fuck. Riley looks awed and amused by her, which I can completely understand. Bree had Flint chasing after her from the moment he laid eyes on her.

Riley quickly gets in her SUV, and after Bree's warning that Flint is close, I pull out behind her as she heads towards town. Curious to see this apartment that Mrs. R gifted her, I grin to myself remembering the look on Riley's face as she inspected my furniture. Seeing how much she loved the puzzle coffee table, I decide to create other pieces for her that will tie into that.

Pulling alongside the curb, directly behind Riley's Jeep, we park in front of a two-story red brick building. The ground floor is an empty storefront with a large window that wraps around the corner of the building, then an entrance for the store and another next to that, which Riley is heading towards.

Reaching over for the measuring tape, I quickly catch up to her and pause to enjoy the view of her ass while she heads upstairs before I lock the lower door behind me. I'm pleased that she has another door to unlock before entering her place. The sun has set by the time we enter, so by the light on her cell, she wanders around hitting switches for overhead lights.

This building is easily eighty to a hundred years old but the apartment looks new and not cheaply done. A birthday present fit for Mrs. R's granddaughter, I think, shaking my head at her family. Newly sanded wood floors flow through a great room that would have been unheard of during the time the building was constructed—a bay window at one end and a new kitchen with an island at the other.

"Come on!" She grabs my hand excitedly, pulling me past a guest room and hallway bath, back to a large master suite. It's larger than the ensuite I call home and I know instantly what her housewarming gift will be. A California King will fit nicely against the long wall, a luxury that I don't have room for at the clubhouse but have already built a bed platform for. I can only gape at the bathroom, never been in anything like it. It has heated floors, a large shower with multiple shower heads and a separate Jacuzzi tub with space for two. Then back through her room, she opens a door that leads to a private deck. I walk across it to make sure that the gate at the top of the stairs leading down to the parking spaces is well secured. It is. Mrs. R's people wouldn't have overlooked that.

"The deck is new," she says, "it's actually a real convenience for the store downstairs. See, you can reverse a truck up to the double doors down there to load and unload without getting rained or snowed on."

Crossing back to her, I decide to address this frankly "Is the whole building yours now? Was that your gift?" I ask, having already guessed the answer.

"Yeah," she almost whispers. "I didn't want to, well, it sounds weird, y'know? Telling, basically, a stranger, that I got a building for my birthday. Gram had me sign the paperwork this morning and someone was there to notarize it, so it's official."

"Basically a stranger?" I grin down at her. "I've already tasted your sweet titties." Riley blushes on cue but slips her arm around me as I pull her inside and secure the back door. "What are you going to do with the store?"

"Well, I have to rent it. I'm responsible for the property tax, insurance and everything else now. Gram gave me a price range for the area, but I, I don't know...would you want to sell from here?" She asks shyly.

I let out the breath I was holding. "Sweetheart, no. Look, I won't take advantage of you. I had contacted some other properties last year but to rent I basically have to show steady business income. And my credit score—well, with the MC, you know I keep a lot of stuff off any books."

"OK, look, I'm going to advertise it but it's been empty since last summer, so even if you decide on month to month you're welcome to it."

Turning the lights off as we walk back towards the front, I shake my head at Mrs. R's antics. Knowing my basic business plans, was this done with me in mind? This feels too much like my G'ma's situation, not that that was bad.

We decide to take my Explorer, so she grabs a duffle from the back of her SUV to get her through our overnight. Calling local hotels, I'm pissed I can't find something nicer for us, but not an easy task during ski season. Driving to an inexpensive chain hotel in silence, I reach out for her hand.

"What are you thinking about, Sweetheart?"

"Just, today was kind of a big day, and I am trying to absorb it all," she murmurs. "Hey! You haven't smoked since I got to the clubhouse?"

"Yeah, been working on that." I look over at her, patting my breast pocket. "I have your lighter right here, but I got the impression you weren't a fan," I say, bringing her hand up to my mouth.

She doesn't say a word for a while, just looks at me with a big smile. "I'm really impressed, Gunner, I've always heard how hard that is to quit. Thank you."

"I still light up sometimes, but pretty much from a pack or two a day to a pack a month," I shrug, trying to ignore the surge of warmth that accompanies her smile.

Tugging her hand away from mine, Riley slides it down and slowly rubs my cock over my jeans. She smiles at me, "Maybe I can distract you so you won't think about smoking?"

"I'm beginning to think you're just using me for sex!" I mockingly accuse her as I pull into the hotel lot. Laughing, she quickly unfastens her seat belt and straddles my lap.

Cupping my face, she gently kisses me. "I want you, but you're right. We have this idea of each other and I know you are trying to protect me by giving us time to rectify the real versus the imagined.

"I appreciate you and do understand we have things to work out, but looking around at the boys on campus and at the idiots my parents paraded me in front of over the holidays, I need you to understand that you are the only one I've ever wanted to jump," my sweetheart says as she caresses the side of my scarred face.

Pulling her to me, I invade her mouth. Sliding my hands down to her ass, I pull her tight against my rock hard cock. I want her more than I've ever wanted anyone. A knock on the window makes us both jump.

There's a rent-a-cop who's yelling about how parking is for hotel guests only and there was a complaint. I open the door into his midsection and tell him we're checking in. Sliding Riley off of me and onto the ground, I follow her after grabbing the bags from the back.

She winds her arm through mine and smiles up at me like she always does. "Let's go talk to my Gram tomorrow, I want to get a better idea of what she's been plotting."

I stop dead in my tracks. A step ahead of me, she gets tugged back at my sudden stop. "Fuck, Sweetheart! No talking about your Gram when I'm hard, OK? I just shrivelled up."

The little witch laughs at me and hurries into the hotel and out of the cold.

RILEY

Standing back and watching him with the security guard and guy working the front desk, they are terrified of him. I know he's huge but I've never felt the least bit threatened nor intimidated by his size, the scar on his face, nor appearance.

Gunner pays for the room and plus an extra incidental charge in cash. He seems to keep clips of it in different pockets so he never pulls out much at any time. I worry about him spending money to make me happy. I felt awful about him paying for the graffiti being removed from my Jeep. And I'll never forget the look on his and Connal's faces at the garage when nearly my whole allowance slid out of my wallet at once. I was so flustered and then embarrassed.

My parents love to show off their wealth and I've always found it obnoxious. My great-grandparents on my mother's side are responsible for most of it and they were what my parents would consider blue collar and beneath them. How hypocritical is that?

I have no room to criticize. I've never worked, I have volunteered with Gram through some of the organizations she's involved with and I always deliver Thanksgiving dinner baskets to those on her church's need list. Really, the best and worst thing my parents ever did for me was have me homeschooled. I was never involved in school cliques but I am so awkward with other people because of not having to deal with that. I've never had a best friend. I have Gram and for a short period of time, I had Ms. Betty, but I never really interacted with people my age. I'm set apart at school now because I am younger than those in my classes. I have access to all of the advantages of wealth without deserving it or getting what I really crave—true interaction with others.

As Gunner motions to me to follow him to our room, I wonder if he REALLY knows what he's in for with me. The one thing Gram has always said to me is to trust my instincts when it comes to people. I know I can't trust my parents, I learned that early on. I know I felt so safe last May when I met Gunner, but in all my musings of him the past year I never considered being spanked. I never thought of it any time I rubbed myself off thinking of him. But holy shit! I was pissed at the first slap, until he softly rubbed my butt then kept going on my count. Now, I'm looking forward to saying sorry some more.

CHAPTER EIGHT

RILEY

"FUCK, RILEY." GUNNER SAYS LOOKING AT ME, AS I FOLLOW him into a space smaller than his room at the clubhouse. "You OK here?"

"I just want to be with you tonight, so yes," I say, trying to sound game about this place. He gathers me in his arms, whispering he has a cabin to take me to tomorrow night.

"You have a cabin nearby?" I ask wondering why we aren't there now.

"It's owned by the MC. It's Hawk's anniversary tonight so he and Anne are there, but I had reserved tomorrow night and can get Monday night also. I just didn't know if you'd skip school."

"I only have two classes on Monday but need to go. Between eleven and three, um, I want to get on top of things for the apartment also." Turning to him as he sits on the bed, I step towards him wanting his hands on me.

"Stop." He holds up his hand keeping me at arm's length. "Strip." This next command terrifies and excites me.

Looking him straight in the eye, I obey. I'd already taken my jacket off, so I kick off my shoes and start with my t-shirt and jeans. Once those are off, I hazard a look up to him. With his nod, I quickly remove my bra and panties. Keeping my arms straight at my sides and nearly shaking with need, standing bare before him I beg for more. "Show me, Gunner."

"Come up here," he motions to the bed beside him. "On all fours, Sweetheart."

I quickly move into position beside him. Still fully dressed, he gently caresses my back, following my curves down my arms, then back around to my bottom. Without warning, he starts spanking me again. Hard and fast, nine slaps later he pauses, gripping me by my hair. As his other hand gently soothes my inflamed skin, he asks for the count.

As I push my ass back into his palm, I moan the number 'nine' and ask him to even it out. In response, he slips a finger into my soaking wet pussy and smears my juices back up to my asshole. "You want to feel me here?" Gunner murmurs into my ear. I freeze as he circles my tight rim with his finger. "I'm gonna claim this too." His voice is rough as he gently pushes against my tightest hole with his thumb. "You still want to be with me?"

"Yes, Gunner," I moan.

He slides his index finger back into my pussy and then pulls his hand back to slap my ass again. "There's your tenth." Pulling my hair back to tug me into him for another kiss, "Gonna be mine, Sweetheart?" He growls into my ear then flips me over.

He stands back to remove his vest and shirt then sitting in a chair near the door, he removes his boots and belt but leaves his jeans on. "Please, Gunner, I want to see all of you!"

Shaking his head, he rejoins me on the bed. He grins

and raises his scarred eyebrow at me as he motions me to move further back up into the pillows. Coming to rest his head in between my thighs, he spreads my legs further to allow for his bulk.

"This little strip for me?" He grins as he traces the remaining tuft of my pubic hair straight down to my clit.

"Yes." I manage to get out before he separates my folds, blowing on that sensitive nub, causing me to arch off the bed. "Please, Gunner!"

"Sensitive!" This will be the last word from him I'm able to comprehend tonight.

GUNNER

I'm quite pleased with myself. I made Ri come so hard she nearly passed out. I didn't know that was possible. Sweetest pussy I ever tasted. I teased and sucked on her clit till she couldn't even say "Please, Gunner" anymore and I managed to work my thumb completely into her asshole. She came hard, squirting all over my face before slumping back. Scared me for a moment, until she moved to curl into me.

Moving away from her and covering her up, I pad to the bathroom to rinse her juices from my face and the light beard that has grown the past couple days. Looking at myself in the mirror as I move to piss, I cannot fathom what she sees in me—shaggy brown hair, blue eyes, complete with partial hearing loss in one ear from the shrapnel that tore up my face. I was never considered good looking and the scar doesn't help much either, but she doesn't seem to care about any of it.

Walking back and easing myself onto the bed next to her, I vow to be good to her. I won't lose her. In sleep, she seems to mirror my thoughts and snuggles tighter against me. The last thought that passes through my mind before sleep overtakes me, is simply 'Mine.'

SLEEPING BETTER THAN I HAD SINCE BEFORE I JOINED THE military, I slowly waken to light kisses and a squirming body under me.

"You're crushing me." Riley giggles quietly, while continuing to scatter kisses across my neck.

Growling, I wrap my arms around her to hold her closer while shifting my weight onto my elbows. Feeling my morning wood against her stomach, she curls her legs around my waist and purrs, "Now have we waited long enough?"

If I didn't have my jeans on, I would bury nine inches of solid wood inside of her. "Not yet, Sweetheart." Kissing her forehead, trying to protect her from morning breath, I move lower against her to suck her tits into my mouth, moving back and forth between each peak and letting them loudly pop out of my mouth. Riley giggles again causing me to frown up at her. "How can anyone be so cheerful when they wake up?"

Smiling down at me, while I switch to flicking her nipples randomly with my tongue, "I'm happy because I woke up to you, to us being together, I guess."

"I've never done that before, you know?" I say, wanting to make her smile even more.

"What?" She looks down at me with a confused look in her eyes.

"I've never spent the night with anyone before," I clarify. Sharply pushing away from me, she slides off the bed without a word and darts to grab my shirt from the floor.

Pulling it over her head, she turns away from me as she realizes the room is too small to put any real distance between us. Standing rigidly, she turns back to me.

"You told me you'd never discuss MC business with me, so I understand that you'll keep some things from me, but you don't get to lie to me. Not under any circumstance!" Gone is my happy Riley, she stands before me furious, with pink cheeks and tears beginning to form in her eyes.

"You're about to get spanked, Sweetheart, and you will not enjoy it this time," I say harshly as I sit up to face this.

"No!" She shouts, standing her ground, "Not when you've lied to me. I won't let you."

"I've never lied to you. I've never spent the night in a bed with anyone. And I remember telling you last year not to question me when I've given my word!" She looks more shocked than angry now, but I cannot stand being called a liar so we're finishing this discussion now. "You won't always like what I tell you, Riley, but you do not get to blow up, calling me a liar. I will not stand for that shit."

The tears that had built up in her eyes spill over as she comes back to me, wrapping her arms around my neck. "I don't understand, Gunner, all the women you've been with? I mean, you...?" She pauses unsure of how to continue.

Sliding my hands in different directions, each securing a cheek, my left arm pulls her lower body more fully into me while I guide her face towards mine with my right hand. "No woman's ever been on the back of my bike nor slept the night in a bed with me, Sweetheart. I don't have many other 'firsts' left, but those two are yours, ours, I mean." I softly kiss her tears away as she sniffles loudly. "You have a bit of temper, don't you, Sweetheart?"

"No, I don't," she breathes out unevenly.

"Yes, you do." I chuckle while contradicting her.

"I don't like being lied to. They used to lie to me about things, making excuses or whatever. Then they stopped even bothering to do that." My anger at her parents flares again when I think of the neglect she faced alone. "I can't tolerate living like that anymore."

"I've sworn an oath to the MC, Riley. Club business doesn't get spoken about with anyone. I swear to you, I won't lie to you or withhold anything personal, anything between us. I won't use my oath to my Brothers to hide things from you, but I won't betray them either."

"What do I say, Gunner? You won't let me say 'sorry' anymore?" She sniffles again.

"Oh, you can say it, Sweetheart. You just know what I'll do when I hear it..." I say laughing at her predicament.

"I won't lie to you either, Gunner." Riley sighs, as she settles herself on my lap. "We won't ever lie to each other." She murmurs more to herself than to me.

Sitting there holding her close with my chin resting on her head, I'm amazed at how quickly I went from angry to content. Tightening my arms around her, loving the feel of her snuggled onto my lap, I grin, deciding to make this her new resting place. Listening to her breathing shift, she stretches up to trace the scar across my face. "Will you tell me what happened?"

Watching her face as she seems to be memorizing the path and texture of the mark, I explain about the patrol through a nothing village in Afghanistan that ended with an IED killing two of my buddies, tearing an arm off another guy, and knocking the shit out of me. Besides the scar, I tell her about the partial hearing loss in my left ear. Her eyes widen and fill with tears again as she moves her finger to trace the outside of my ear.

"Thank you for your service," she says, looking back to

my eyes. As I lower my mouth to kiss hers, I hear the loudest rumble I have ever heard from another human being and freeze for a moment realizing it's coming from her stomach! I jerk and nearly unseat her as she blushes furiously and grabs her stomach.

"How is that coming from you?" I sputter, laughing, while I stand us up to get dressed. "Guess I need to feed that beast!"

"You!" She laughs and smacking at my arms with her tiny hand before turning to pull on her jeans. "I was too nervous to eat much yesterday and now I'm too embarrassed!"

"You should be!" I can't help but continue to tease her. "I've lived with Marines and Bikers and have never heard anything like that!"

"Oh Come On!" Riley mock yells at me. "It wasn't that bad!" Then she gets the upper hand by removing my shirt and tossing it to me. As I stand, staring at this beautiful—naked—woman, she laughs at herself as she digs through her duffel bag for a fresh shirt. "But I think today will be Special #6 day if we go to Ray's." She smiles at the now shocked look on my face.

"There's no way you can put away the #6!" I ordered it once and barely finished it. Full stack of pancakes, 3 eggs, cheesy hash browns, plus a couple pieces each of bacon and sausage.

"Want to bet?" She's gotta be shitting me, she's like 5'4" and only curvy where she should be.

"You're on. What's the prize?" I rake my eyes up and down her body.

Looking way to innocent, she pretends to think about it. "Winner gets dessert tonight." This girl is killing me. Sealing it with a kiss, we get going.

CHAPTER NINE

GUNNER

HEADING INTO THE DINER, I'M SURPRISED TO SEE HOW FULL IT is. Not nearly as surprised as the patrons seeing Riley and me together though.

Margie, a waitress who's worked here forever, nearly trips over her feet when she sees us sliding into a booth together. She stops to get a Diet Coke on the way over which Riley eagerly reaches for. I've already positioned my coffee mug for my first jolt of the day.

"Honey, everything alright?" Margie asks Riley. I've been coming here for years, yet Marge is looking between Riley and me like I've kidnapped her. Worse still, she is waiting on Riley's response before pouring my coffee.

"I'm great Margie, how's your grandson doing?" Riley jumps in like there's nothing out of the ordinary happening. Marge starts to calm down as she replies. moments later she remembers to get our order and finally pours my coffee. Riley goes all in with the #6, how could I do any less?

RILEY

I can't help but laugh as Gunner groans again. He won't admit it but he's a little sick from the breakfast. I was epically hungry and won the bet. I can put food away when I have a mind to.

Gram had plans after church this morning so she put off having Gunner and me stop by.

Gunner and me. I grin to myself as I look over at him. Pulling up the drive to my parents' home, I let him know, again, that he's welcome to come in and wait while I pack some things. Giving me the same dark look as the first time I asked, I'll know he'll be waiting in his truck.

Heading up to the attic, I decide to pull out three large bags instead of a duffle bag. I am going to be moving to the apartment as soon as possible so I may as well start moving things since Gunner is here to help. I haphazardly empty my dresser into two of the bags and start grabbing my favorite clothes from the closet, happy to leave behind the Lilly Pulitzer/Stepford Wives casual wear and other formal attire my mother bought, insisting I needed. I call Gunner to ask him to get the bags from the top of the main stairs. I know I'll topple down if I try to carry them. He groans but agrees to help.

An hour later, we've secured the bags in my new apartment and are heading to the grocery store. After a crack about keeping me well fed, Gunner goes in to pick up food for the next couple days. Heading further up the mountain, our conversation flows easily about movies, food, him telling me more about his Brothers in the MC and what drew him in. His easy conversation contradicts so many ideas of what I would have expected a biker to be like but know that they reflect his grandmother's influence in his life.

I can't help but think how we experienced two sides of a coin. And try not to fail miserably when I verbalize it. "So, my parents were together and wealthy, and I would have loved to have been raised by my Gram. Your parents were not together and didn't, well, had limited means," I stumble a bit there. "But you were ultimately raised by your grandmother, who sounds wonderful. You see our common ground, right?"

"Shitty parents?"

I can't help but laugh. "Gunner, I don't usually swear, but yes. Shitty parents!"

"How'd you think we'd do as parents?" He asks, focusing on the road ahead of him.

Snapping my head around to look at him. "Hey! I want to finish school and start working."

Reaching out for my hand, Gunner brings it to his lips. "OK, so it'll be a few years for us, I can understand that, but I'd be open to knocking you up."

"Wow. Thanks," I laugh at him. "What an offer! At least we'd know what not to do with a child, right?"

"When it's time, we'll do it right. I can't imagine you being anything but a great mom," he says, making my ovaries flutter.

"I, well, we haven't talked about it," I say while hugging his hand against my chest, "I just started on birth control. I tried one type but didn't react well to it, then had to wait a week to get on a lower hormone version. Can you, I mean, when we do it, can you use a condom?"

"I've never done it unwrapped, I get tested once a year and am clean. I can get you whichever pill you like, if that's what you want," he assures me.

"What, you have a stockpile of birth control?" I can't help but quirk an eyebrow at him over that statement.

"They have it at the clubhouse. You know, for the Girlies. Tell me what is best for you and if we don't have it, I'll pay you back for it. OK?" Gunner notices my silence at the mention of the girls who hang around the MC members. Exhaling deeply, he squeezes my hand but doesn't say anything further. The Girlies will definitely be a conversation I'll have with Bree.

We continue in an easy silence the rest of the way to the cabin. There's a truck in the drive and we pull in beside it. Gunner looks over at me, "Looks like Hawk and Anne are still around. We good?"

I nod and lean over to kiss him, "We're good. Um, do you and Hawk get along?" I've heard so many names and nicknames the past day that I can barely keep up.

"Yeah Sweetheart, we're good. He and Anne dated all through high school and she waited for him while he served. She's a tough one, but I can't imagine you not getting along. I'll come back out for the food and bags later." He gets out and comes around the front of the vehicle as I hop out. He pushes me back up along the side of the truck, dipping his head down to my neck.

"That's not how that works, Sweetheart." He murmurs, lightly biting my neck.

I'm immediately breathless but manage to moan something that sounds like a question. "When we're in a cage, I get your door." He punctuates the sentence by nipping my earlobe. "Should I punish you if you forget?"

"I think you may need to," I can't help but smile up at him and hold him tighter as he pulls back.

"Gunner, Jesus Christ, stop mauling the girl and get your ass in here and out of the cold!" That has to be Hawk. He's gorgeous. Probably a foot shorter than Gunnar and slim. Looking at his bone structure I imagine he's at least part Native American. His long, straight black hair is offset by piercing light blue eyes and a light caramel tone to his skin. His easy smile welcomes us as Gunner tells him to fuck off before giving me a little tug to start towards the cabin.

"Pretty Girl, am I happy to meet you, but what the hell are you doing with this ugly, old guy?!" I narrow my eyes and briefly consider kicking Hawk's shin until I see the ready laugh in his eyes. I reach out to take his outreached hand.

"Hi, I'm Riley. I can't help myself, his frown gets me all worked up!" I quip, getting a hip check from Gunner and a hearty laugh from Hawk.

As we enter, I see a woman almost as tall as Hawk off to the side, already taking my measure. Her short hair is almost as blond as Hawks is dark. Unable to stop my eyes, they go straight to a large strawberry mark on the right side of her face, starting near her brown eyes and curving along her cheek and back to her ear. I quickly, and guiltily, look up to her eyes. She rolls them, indicating a very solid 'whatever'.

Closing the space between us, I hold my hand out, "Hi, Anne, right? I'm Riley." With a tight smile that isn't reflected in her eyes, she returns my acknowledgement with a nod and shakes my hand.

"How long have you been with her, Gunner?" She asks, looking over my shoulder. Gunner mentioned she was tough, I'm wondering if that was code for bitch.

Before he can answer, I say, "Since yesterday." She looks back to further assess me as I turn to Hawk. "I hope we didn't show up to early, my Gram was tied up so we just thought we'd head up after we ran some errands."

Both Gunner and Hawk look thoroughly amused as they take in Anne's power play and my dismissal of it. Seriously, she has nothing on my parents, their friends, nor the demonic offspring of their friends, who I have been forced to spend time with.

"Your Gram lives around here?" Hawk throws in to fill the void while motioning to the sofas. Gunner sits down first and as I move to sit beside him, he grabs my hips to pull me onto his lap. Hawk laughs as I shriek. Anne sits in a lounger across from us looking less than amused. I curl into Gunner, happy to have his support in the face of Anne's perusal.

"Oh yeah, she's lived here most her life. We wanted to visit, but that is one busy lady so we'll probably wait till Friday when I usually see her." I am babbling, I know it, but can't stop.

"No, I'll see her Tuesday," Gunner interjects, getting similar looks of surprise from all of us. Looking annoyed at this he looks down at me. "It's my monthly visit with her, I told you."

"I know you did, but I didn't know it was this Tuesday," I reply, almost forgetting that Hawk and Anne are here. "I have class and can't go."

"So her Grandmother introduced you two?" Anne jumps in, trying to figure out how we crossed paths.

"No," Gunner and I say at the same time. Letting Gunner continue, "But her Gram and my grandmother were long-time friends and I have a standing monthly visit with her since I came back."

"You're in school?" Hawk interjects.

"Oh, do you go to high school down in town?" Anne just won't let up. Gunner gently tightens his arms around me.

"Nope. I'm nearly a junior over at the university. I just

changed my major but still think I can graduate in two more years." Anne narrows her eyes again. "Do you work, Anne?"

"I have a jewelry and accessory line," she slowly replies, as though trying to figure out her next barb.

Hawk takes over, "It's doing great. It's carried at several places in town and has a great following on Etsy."

"Really? What's it called?" I ask to be polite.

Her response momentarily startles me. Then I pull my hair back to show earrings from her collection.

"I love these!" Showing the little lightning bolts. "I also have two boxes of the ten single earrings and really only take these out when I mix and match those!" The tide has turned. Gunner must agree as he has loosened his hold on me.

"Those are for people with multiple piercings, of course, but it's great that you wear different earrings together." She leans forward in her seat and asks about my degree program. While interacting with a less hostile Anne, I notice Hawk watching Gunner and me together. I'm at ease on Gunner's lap and he gently rubs my back with one arm as I mindlessly run my fingers along his other arm.

"So, what did you think of the clubhouse, Riley?" Hawk asks, trying to get a read on us.

"She...um, you went to the club?" Anne asked surprised. "Were you lost?"

"It was interesting," I respond, looking up at Gunner as he frowns at Hawk. Silence ensues, but Anne isn't done with this yet.

"Gunner, what was she doing there?"

Dropping a quick kiss on my forehead, he looks me in the eyes. "Coming for me," he replies. I sigh and smile up at him like the besotted school girl Anne judged me to be upon arrival.

Understanding that we aren't going to feed their curiosity today, Hawk stands and gestures around the cabin.

"We changed the sheets this morning. The dryer is still going so if we could leave that to you to deal with? We gotta be picking up the kids from Anne's sister, so, nice to meet you, Riley. Gunner, come check this out." He indicates a deck and they walk out leaving Anne and me alone.

"There's a lot of competition for him, you know?" Anne says pointedly. "I've told my sister to give it up, but she hasn't listened. They hooked up once. Then one of the Girlies thought, well, never mind that, she's a bitch anyway."

"I'm sure she won't be the only bitch I cross paths with while we figure this out," I reply, not backing down.

Anne looks at me dead on, then her shoulders start to lightly shake, next thing she's laughing outright as she approaches me.

"Oh, I may just like you yet!" She announces as she kisses me on the check. "Don't you let him walk all over you, understand?"

I nod, hesitantly smiling. "Um, your sister and Gunner?" Not sure how to ask about that, she quickly cocks her head at me.

"Nearly two years ago. From what I've heard, he hasn't been with anyone in a while though."

I try to keep from looking pleased but I doubt she misses anything. Gunner and Hawk come back inside, and gathering their things Hawk and Anne head out. As Gunner secures the door, I dramatically throw myself onto the couch. "'Tough' Gunner? You said she was tough, not to expect the Spanish Inquisition."

Crossing the room, he quickly lifts me over his shoulder and sets off down a hallway. Tossing me onto a bed, he growls, “Take your clothes off now.” Surprised, I lie there watching him strip. “Now, Riley!”

Shaking my head, “I won the bet earlier. It’s my turn, Gunner. Show me.” I purr at him. Where did this girl who purrs at a giant come from? I wonder, smiling up at him.

Kicking his boots off, he then peels his jeans and shirt off before he reaches over grabbing the back of my head and pulling it against his crotch, covered only in boxers. “This what you want, Sweetheart?” He asks gruffly. “You better be hungry. You were wiggling that sweet ass against my cock for the past twenty minutes and I have zero patience left.”

“Teach me,” I reply. Wasting no more time, Gunner removes his boxers and sits up against the headboard.

“No teeth, Riley. Start at the tip. Rhythm is key.”

CHAPTER TEN

RILEY

Holding the base of his semi-hard cock, I dart my tongue out to circle its head. A sharp intake of breath followed by a drop of pre-cum intrigue me enough to pull back and study his length further. I've seen pictures of penises in my med classes, granted Gunner is huge physically, so his well-proportioned cock shouldn't come as any surprise. It's pretty intimidating to me all at once.

"It'll fit, Sweetheart. It'll fit everywhere I want to put it," he says, reading my mind. The look he is giving me sets me on fire.

Leaving the pre-cum in place, I push his cock up towards his stomach a bit. Then starting at the base, I slowly slide my tongue up its length. Making eye contact with him when I reach the end is one of the most empowering moments of my life. His eyes are half-mast and desperate with need.

I enclose the end of his cock with my lips while finally licking away Gunner's pre-cum with the tip of my tongue.

Not breaking the seal of my lips, I start moving them up and down while simultaneously working my hand in the same rhythm.

Propped on my elbow, I reach my left hand down and gently massage his balls. So much of my saliva has pooled down there, I quickly distribute the moisture around and they steadily harden as I caress them.

Gunner's hands had been tightly fisted in the blanket on either side of his body but now reach up to thread through my hair. Using them to hasten my speed, he starts a low keening sound followed by the word 'Fuck' over and over again. Pushing me back, "I'm gonna cum, Sweetheart, you don't have to..."

He doesn't get another word out before I plunge back onto his cock and renew sucking him, harder than before. With a final bellow, he blows in my mouth and I swallow every last drop. Tangy, like I'd heard, musky even, but nothing cringe-worthy like I half expected. I pull my mouth back but dart my tongue out to get the last squirt that comes out, causing Gunner to groan again.

Smiling like the Cheshire Cat, I plant a kiss on either of his thighs then move up along his body. He secures me fiercely to his chest while stroking my hair.

"Sweetheart?" Gunner whispers as he turns into me, looking entirely too serious and overly innocent. "You'll need lots of practice, but that was a good start."

Giving him my harshest glare, I quickly reply, "Maybe I should find someone to practice on?" That's barely out of my mouth before Gunner pins me to the bed. With the last rays of daylight coming in through the window next to us, I find myself staring into the face of a wild animal looking at his next meal.

"No. One. Else." He growls, holding my arms above my head. "I know I sound like a goddamn psycho right now, but you're mine. Just mine. Let me hear you say it."

Stunned by the nearly feral look I see in his eyes, I squirm beneath him. As he releases my wrists, I quickly cup his cheeks. "We've been here before, Gunner. I knew I wanted you when we met and I know I want you now, but you can't ask for that and not swear the same to me. I want all of you. From now on, I mean, just mine. You cheat on me and I'll never let you touch me again."

"We make this promise to each other, we make it now and I'll claim you sooner than I planned. I...you...Sweetheart, you're getting the shit end of this deal. You want to sleep on it?" His elbows are supporting his weight as he holds himself above me.

"I'm scared, Gunner." I had opened my mouth meaning to swear myself to him, but I am terrified of trusting my happiness to anyone. "Are you sure about being with me?"

"Riley, I don't want anyone else but you. I haven't had a relationship in my adult life but from the time you looked up at me at the car wash, that's been it for me, Sweetheart. I should have walked away from you but I'm a selfish bastard.

"My past will be thrown at you around the MC. I have fucked a lot of women I didn't give a shit about. I have beaten and killed men. I live in the grey area of this world, and that will be cast on you too. But, I'm consumed by this connection I feel to you, if you need time to figure it out, I get that." He pauses, lying back on his side next to me before whispering. "But I'm all in. I will be faithful to you."

"I'm yours, Gunner. Just yours," I say with certainty, curling back into him. "But I'm still scared."

GUNNER

I am being selfish, but that's another flaw of mine she seems determined to overlook. I never cease to be surprised by Riley standing up to me or throwing my sarcasm back at me; it's the absolute rage that surges through me when I think of her touching or being touched by another man that I can barely rectify with myself.

She's right to be scared, I am too.

Enjoying the peace of holding her in my arms, I'm loathe to get outta bed but nature calls. Coming out of the adjoined bathroom I'm disappointed that she's no longer in bed. Looking around, I remember the bags left in the Explorer.

Heading back to the main room, I go to join Riley in the kitchen as she unpacks the groceries.

"Gunner, do you want dinner? Otherwise, I might throw together a snack." She's got to be kidding. I'm still full from breakfast. I know I'm staring at her with my jaw open, but I don't know where she packs this food away.

"Sweetheart? Don't get mad or anything, but you aren't bulimic or something like that, are you?"

She turns away, starting to blush again, but says something about a fast metabolism. Closing the distance between us, I wrap my arms around her. "I'm fine for right now. Besides, I want to cook for you. I can do steak and asparagus on the grill, ok?"

"Won't you freeze out there? We can just cook in here tonight..." I'm shaking my head at her.

"Nope, besides, I can get the hot tub started up while I'm out at the grill. You game for a dip after dinner?"

"I've never been in one, how can that possibly be fun in

this weather?" Riley has her nose wrinkled up at the thought. I can't believe she grew up in the mountains and has never been in a hot tub. "Besides, I don't have a suit with me."

"Now we're definitely going in the hot tub! No suit needed, Sweetheart, just you and me up here." I laugh at her shocked expression. The idea of skinny dipping seems to freak her out more than me spanking her. More than ever, I want her to get used to being naked when we're alone together. I go to poke the fire that Hawk had going before we arrived.

As the fire starts to build up again, I turn to see that Riley has followed me out carrying two beers. She looks shyly at me as if waiting for a nod about drinking underage. I merely reach for mine, clinking it against her bottle. She doesn't need my permission, and I rather she learns that on her own than looking for approval. Riley follows me as I move to sit on the sofa.

"Take your pants off, Sweetheart, I'll keep you warm." I stop her before she sits, holding her bottle out to me. She complies without hesitation, making me smile.

Pulling her onto my lap and I pull a blanket around us. She squirms around until she's comfortable then smiles up at me.

"You know, except for the restaurants, every time I try to sit you pull me onto your lap!"

"I like you here, so get used to it," I growl at her, but she laughs at me so I stop trying to hide my grin as I take a swallow of beer.

"It might even be more fun if your jeans were off also?" She throws at me, curling into my chest again and staring into the fire.

"Always want your way, don't you?" As Riley looks momentarily hurt, I soften it with a kiss and change the subject. "So among the many things I don't know, what foods don't you like?"

The next hours are spent talking and snuggled together except for bathroom breaks and beer refills. She's smart and reads a lot about world events, so while young, makes interesting points and even though we don't agree on everything. I mirror her attitude of 'even if I don't agree with you on a subject, I'll respect your right to your opinion.' And hell, at eighteen, she's able to explain her reasoning behind her opinions in a way that I couldn't at that age, while staying open to any counter-points I make.

In what seems like no time at all, I hear her stomach rumble and drop a kiss on her cheek before shifting her so I can get the food started. She sets the table while I prepare everything on the grill and make good on my promise to start up the heater on the hot tub. When I'm ready to sit down, I notice she has laid out some terry-cloth robes and has changed into one of the shirts from my bag. Brushing past her, I snake my hand under the bottom hem to confirm that she's trying to hide her commando status beneath the size of my shirt.

"Hey!" Riley squeals up at me as I goose her. Moving to take her seat she pouts in my direction, "I'm starving. No playing till after I eat my body weight!"

I laugh along with her, pleased she doesn't mind making fun of herself. "I'm not playing, Sweetheart. But I do want to know why you're sitting so far from me?" I shift our plates over to the side of the table that has a farmhouse style bench. "I'd have thought you noticed I like you right up next to me."

The meal starts off pretty quiet, she really is hungry

again. "There's something I was wondering about." She's majorly hesitant about whatever she wants to ask. "Um, I know that you guys transport drugs, but I was wondering if you, well, if you..."

Helping her out, I jump in with what I think she's trying to ask. "I don't. I used to smoke pot but not really since the Corps. It always made me a little sick. Nothing harder than liquor, you'll see that I like to be in control. I'd be giving that up if I did."

She's noticeably relieved, but I carry on. "Some of the guys do, they can do whatever in their own time as long as it doesn't interfere with MC business. Jas won't allow anything stronger than weed at the clubhouse, so please don't tell me you're hiding a meth addiction?" I say, grinning over at her as I polish off my steak.

"Meth? Gunner, I'm rich, I'm into the good stuff!" Riley laughs, throwing a wink at me to show she's back to being a smart ass.

"The good stuff? Did you just throw that out cause you weren't sure what sounded expensive and hardcore?"

Nodding at me, she's quick to give up trying to come across as a badass. "Pretty much."

"Are you done, Sweetheart?" I can't wait anymore. Getting a shy nod in reply, "Leave the plates and come on." I lead her towards the door to the deck, scooping up the robes on the way. Moving quickly to the hot tub, I shuck my jeans and boxers and slide in. The night air hastens Riley forward when she looks like she'd rather drag her feet. Taking a deep breath, she slips my shirt over her head and follows me in the wonderfully hot water.

"Give it a minute, Sweetheart. Your head won't feel cold at all." Trying to pull her back up against my chest, she quickly slips my grasp and turns to straddle me. My cock jerks up between us and I can't help but groan as I lean down to kiss her full lips.

Her reaction to me each time I kiss her is instantaneous and overwhelming. Riley gives herself up to me with each kiss, with each touch. No half measures, no pretending, no going through the motions like so many of the women I've been with. I feel so much hope, trust, and passion coming from her in our kiss that I break free from her. I pull her tight to my chest hoping she won't question me. I have no answers for her now.

She's giving me exactly what I want but I don't deserve it, any of it, and certainly not from her.

I push her back as I stand and reach for our robes, "Come on, get inside. Why don't you take the room we were in before? I'll take the other one and can drive you back in the morning." I toss over my shoulder as I'm getting out of the hot tub.

I have to walk away from her, she deserves more than me. I can't be this much of a bastard, not when it comes to her.

Realizing she hasn't moved, I turn towards her but don't raise my eyes to her face, knowing I couldn't stand to see her in pain. She turns her back to me, arms crossing to cover her chest.

"You're a liar and coward," she chokes out, choosing to remain in the hot water. At this moment, she is right and I've never felt so ashamed of myself.

RILEY

I can't move. I can barely breathe. In less than two days he promised me everything then changed his mind. About us.

I know Gunner hasn't moved from the doorway but I

want him to. I want him gone so I don't have to shame myself by showing him all of me again, of him seeing the horror of his rejection on my face.

"Riley," he starts then pauses and I hear the rustle of the robe. "I'm not right for you. You deserve so much more than me. Please understand. This is me trying to do the best thing for you." I can't contain the sob that escapes me. I cover my mouth, mortified at exposing myself as weak.

Feeling his hands slide in to tug me out of the water, he murmurs, "Come on, you should come inside, Sweetheart." Hearing the endearment from his lips, I lose it.

I spin towards him, kicking off with my foot against the seat, which in addition to his pull increases my momentum and before I can register anything he is flat on his back as I'm hitting him for all I'm worth. I don't register the cold against my naked, wet skin nor the pain from hitting what must be an iron jaw. All I can feel is disappointment throughout my very soul.

It must take a moment for him to catch his breath from the fall but when he does, he wraps his arms tightly around me and though I fight to break free, I am powerless to move until he allows it. He loosens his grip and rolls to get his knees under him. His groan reaches my ears but doesn't register as I start to realize I am freezing. He lifts me into his arms, moaning.

"Fuck. You do have a temper, Sweetheart. Don't sell yourself short."

"Don't say that. Don't call me that ever again." I can't stop the tears now that my anger has started to dissipate. "Cold. So cold," is all I can get out through my chattering teeth. "Please."

Kicking the door closed behind us, Gunner carries me to the back bedroom for the second time today. Standing me long enough to pull back the covers, he settles me in the bed then lays half on top of me as he gathers the blankets around us. My breath is still shaky as warmth slowly creeps back into me. I hold myself stiff as a board while he caresses my hair. When he finally speaks, I can barely make out the words.

"I have done some truly fucked up things in my life, Riley. You deserve so much more than me." He pauses and I refuse to say anything. "I meant every word I said to you, but how can I ever be right for you?"

"By trusting me enough to believe I know what's right for me." Sighing, I will myself to stay strong through my next thought. "You told me you'd never lie to me and that you were all in, did you mean it, even a little?" I ask, staring him down.

"Riley, Sweetheart?" He gives me his lopsided little grin as he slides in his endearment for me again. "In the hot tub, with you all up against me? The last time I felt that way, I was nineteen, halfway around the world, we were pinned down with bullets flying and guys dying." He pauses again and then whispers, "I'm so fucking terrified of you. Of what I feel for you. I didn't run then and I am so sorry I tried to run from you."

I put my finger over his lips, "Did you just say 'sorry'?" I ask, narrowing my eyes at him.

"Let me finish, Sweetheart." He kisses my finger before continuing. "I know I'm asking for a lot of faith after what I just did. I shut down and started to run, I didn't try to talk to you about what I felt. You did that much for me when you got upset at the hotel earlier. From now on, I'll talk. I'm not used to it but I will try."

I feel so vulnerable at this moment. I need to process his earlier reaction but don't want to leave the comfort I find in his arms. Turning my back towards him, I simply say, "Let's sleep on it," and lie quietly beside his tense body. I work to calm my breathing and he eventually relaxes, folding his arms around me and nuzzling the back of my head. My mind is whirling but overstressed, I drift off mid-thought.

CHAPTER ELEVEN

RILEY

BARELY CRACKING AN EYE, I SEE ENOUGH TO CONFIRM WHAT I felt as the veil of sleep was easing back and forcing me into the new day.

"That's really creepy," I say, with both eyes firmly shut again.

"What?" Gunner asks in a nearly hoarse voice.

"How long have you been staring at me?" I roll to burrow my face into his neck, only then remembering we're both naked. And he chuckles.

"How is that creepy? You're so beautiful, Riley," he says, laying a kiss on top of my head. "You looked content, and when I moved your hair off your face you smiled." Deciding not to care that we're naked and there's a sword pressing into my hip, I cuddle closer.

"Sweetheart?" Gunner says while placing soft kisses across my forehead, "I fucked up last night."

"You mean to say, you're sorry?" I totally get to screw with him over this...

"I do not like being spanked, or a number of other things that I like to be on the giving end of."

"Fine. Then we call it a 'get out of jail free card.' There'll be a time you want to spank me and you can't because I'll call it in." I murmur, raising my right leg up to circle his hip, stunned when he moves my leg back down and holds me away from him.

The intensity of his dark blue gaze makes me want to move back into him, annoying me that he's holding me away. "Are we okay, Riley? Please tell me what an ass I am, but that we're okay?"

"We're one for one in the momentary freak out department." I point out. "The difference is, Gunner, you don't get to unilaterally decide what's best for me ever again." Barely whispering my feelings, I focus on tracing one of his tattoos rather than see his face. "You almost destroyed me last night."

"There may be other aspects of our life where I make a call before discussing it with you first, but no more trying to push you away. I will become someone you deserve, I swear it." For once, it's Gunner who's stumbling over words. I exhale feeling confident again. "Is it safe to call you 'Sweetheart' again?"

"Don't get a big head, but it makes me feel like I've been hugged every time you call me that."

"Look at me, Riley." I do, but before he can continue, the morning light across his face brings a cry from my lips.

"Gunner, NO!" He is totally startled and nearly falls off the bed as he whips his head around, as though looking for an intruder.

"What?"

"You have a black eye!" I am mortified.

"Well, yeah, from your tiny fists last night." He grins like this happens every day, but seeing the evidence of my fury causes me to start crying again. At this rate, I'll be severely dehydrated if we stay together.

He rolls over on top of me, all the while trying to soothe me. "I deserved that, Sweetheart. Don't cry anymore, please Riley?"

I wrap my arms and legs around his body, leaning up to kiss the reminder from last night. "I didn't mean to, I've never hit anyone on purpose before."

"Well, then, you're kind of a badass, Sweetheart. I am thoroughly impressed." Gunner is grinning down at me. Dropping his gaze to my chest, he leans down to kiss along my collarbone before asking permission to continue. "There was something I was planning on doing, before I screwed up last night..."

"Oh, yeah?" I murmur, smoothing down his hair with my hands. "What's that?" I tighten my legs around his waist, grinding my clit against his boner.

"Shhh, I'll show you if you behave..." He moves to unwind my legs from around him, pushing me flat onto the bed. As he rolls my rock hard nipples between his rough fingers, I can't help but moan and arch my hips back up at him. Giving me that devastating smile of his, he glides his hand over the curve of my stomach and teasingly tip-toes his fingers down over my clit, dipping his index finger into my wet pussy. Groaning as he playfully nips my breast, he scoops out the moisture he finds within me.

Moving his hand back up to dab my cream around my nipples; keeping eye contact with me as he slowly licks them clean, he dips his finger into my mouth. "See how good you taste, Sweetheart?"

Unable to deny him, I open my mouth and suck on his

finger. Wishing for another appendage in my mouth, I reach down to grab his cock. "No, Riley. Not yet."

Holding my hands to my sides, he slides further down, darting his tongue out to lazily swipe through my slit until he finds my clit. Sucking that into his mouth he continues to torture me until I can't form any thoughts, then draws back, lying beside me.

"Gunner, please don't stop. I need you," I beg.

"I know, come up on here." He half lifts me until my nearly dripping pussy is hovering over his face. "Ride me. You set the pace now, Ri."

And I do. My ass cheeks are secured in each of his hands as he holds me in place and I grind down on his tongue and nose until I'm so close to coming I lose all coordination. Then he takes over for me, keeping my pace while sucking and nipping my clit harder and harder as pleasure and pain all jumble together to push me over the edge. I scream indistinguishable words.

Finally slumping against the wall in front of me, I eventually register the rumbling I feel as his laughter. Crumbling to his side, I feel nervous and exposed. Looking at him, my cum has coated his face. "You are a squirter," Riley.

"Is that bad?" I've never heard that term, and while he looks pleased with himself, I'm still new to all of this.

"Sweetheart, I'm two for two making you squirt. Considering I thought squirting was an urban legend that makes you a unicorn. My very own unicorn." Gunner looks pretty smug as he wipes his hand down his face, bringing it back up to take a sniff followed by a lick. "So delicious." Looking over at my red face that I'm trying to hide while I figure this out, he rolls towards me, pulling me close.

"Don't be shy," he snuggles his head into the crook of my

neck, whispering directly into my ear. "It really turns me on that I can make you feel that good."

I don't have my phone nearby and am too embarrassed to ask the difference between coming and squirting, but know I'll be running a search on that the first chance I get. "I want to make you cum now, Gunner." I peek up at him, kissing his chin then rubbing my nose in his light covering of whiskers.

"Don't think I don't want it, but you have to shower!"

"What?!"

"School day, Sweetheart. And I have some stops to make. I'll drop you off at school, what time for your pick up?" He asks as he maneuvers us off the bed.

"No, just take me to my car and we can meet back here later," I suggest, trying to make it easier for him. "You have it for another night, right?"

"I do, but I'm driving you. Go get ready and I'll start breakfast."

Groaning and moving slowly to the bathroom, I get a little more excited thinking about breakfast. Planning out my day while in the shower, I decide to get the utilities transferred over to my name during my break in between classes, and then I will hit the superstore later to get basics for the apartment. The threat of having to shop should be enough to convince Gunner to drop me at my SUV. Dressing and gathering what I'll need for the day, I head to the kitchen.

"I made breakfast sandwiches, you ok eating on the road?"

Wiping some crumbs from his short whiskers, I kiss him softly. "Sure, what do you have planned for today?" Wondering what the rush is as we head to his Explorer.

"I decided on a housewarming present for you, then I have to check in at the MC after that. You ok at school until two or three? I'll text you when I'm heading to get you."

"Gunner, first, you don't have to buy me anything! You got me a birthday helmet that I love. Secondly, I need to buy stuff for the apartment. I mean like, go to the superstore-and-fill-two-carts up type of shopping. You can just take me to my SUV, ok?"

"Sweetheart," he says, opening the door for me and grabbing my butt as he gives me a boost into his truck. "I want to spend as much time as I can with you today and tomorrow. I've got a short trip that'll start Wednesday, so I am willing to be tortured while you shop. And the gift is as much for me as it is for you, so that's non-negotiable."

After getting in, he leans in for a kiss as I ask, "Where are you going?"

Leaning back without delivering my kiss, he says, "Club business." And starts his truck as I sit waiting for any other details. None are forthcoming.

"When will you be back?" I try next.

"I'm not sure."

"Is this what it'll be like? Do you get to call me from the road?" I ask, not trying to pick a fight but genuinely curious.

"This is it, this is what I do. I will text you if I can but no calls." He holds himself stiffly, waiting for my reaction. I reach over and lay my hand on his thigh.

"I changed my mind about something earlier and didn't get a chance to tell you." I didn't think he could get any more tense, but he did as he tries to figure out what I mean. "I decided I hate it when you tell me, or you use the word deserve. So I'm changing my get out of jail free word from when you say 'sorry' to when you say 'deserve'. Got it?"

GUNNER

I almost drove off the goddamn road when she starts out saying she changed her mind. Fuck, I held it together long enough to hear her out and when she explains, my asshole finally un-puckers and I can breathe again.

"Fuck, Riley. Don't do that to me, Sweetheart." I whisper, knowing I have to get used to her being a smart ass.

"What? I'm serious. I hate it when you talk like I should be on a pedestal and try to negate how happy you make me." I reply, ignoring any reference to how I scared him.

Placing my hand on top of hers and finally smiling again, I can't help but tease her. "But sometimes you really DESERVE a spanking, Riley. Can't I say that?"

"Ha, no. Especially not when you get that look in your eye! Like you want to strangle me. Come to think of it, if you're already looking at me like that, does that mean our 'honeymoon period is over?" She blinks innocently.

Laughing, "Let me rephrase that then, 'you're going to get a spanking tonight, Riley.' Is that better?"

"Gunner! I was teasing you. And about the other thing, you told me about not being able to talk about club business. I get it, I just wanted to know more about what to expect and if I can get ahold of you if I need to. I wasn't pushing you for information." She squeezes my hand to let me know she's sincere.

Exhaling and nodding in reply to her explanation, I'm again floored at how accepting she is of me and my lifestyle. Approaching the campus, I stop to check in at the guard hut and shake my head at Ronnie, the guy I know who hangs out at our MC from time to time. Don't want to get into our connection with Riley right now, and thankfully he plays along. I get directions from her about where to drop her off and where I can find her later, then head out.

CHAPTER TWELVE

GUNNER

My first stop in town is the mattress store. It's fucking ridiculous, all the kinds of mattresses they have, I finally chose a medium firm one and pay extra to get the California King delivered the next day. I may be leaving town for a few days but I want Riley to be able to stay at her new place and not go back to the house she was raised in.

Next, I head towards the clubhouse. It's surprisingly dead. Betsy, one of the Girlies, is upfront cleaning and quietly greets me.

"Who's in back?" I ask, stopping to get a Coke at the bar.

"Jas came in a little while ago. It was crazy here last night so I don't know if Vice is up yet. Where've you been Gunner?" She asks giving me a smile and a wink. "Deb's been keeping an eye out..."

"I'm taken now, Betsy, so knock that shit off and tell the others," I growl as I walk past her, not missing the shocked expression on her overly made-up face. It occurs to me I haven't seen Riley in makeup yet.

Heading back to Jasper's office, I knock even as I'm walking through the door. He's alone and does not look happy.

"Good. Gotta talk to you. Sit the fuck down," he starts.

"What's up, Boss?" Expecting fallout from hitting Frank, it actually turns out to be worse.

"Someone's skimming. I know Flint was always good with the books and I either need him to check these out or get someone voted in as Treasurer."

"Yeah, but we can't get anyone in as Treasurer until we know who's cheating us," I put in, addressing the downside first.

"Bingo. And why the Fuck did you hit Frank? I didn't need to hear about that shit on top of dealing with this." He grins at me, letting me know he doesn't give a shit that Frank got hit.

"He touched my...my Riley. I was out of line, I'll talk to him." I quickly concede defeat about that topic.

"You claim someone I don't know about, Gunner? Then we will have a big fucking problem." Jas sits back in his chair.

"Not yet. I'm going to claim her in the next month or so, depending on how we are. I was going to talk to you today. Can I lay it out?" At his nod, I start to tell him the short version. Including whom her family is and that she came here the other day not knowing the score and that lead to Frank thinking she was fair game. Before I can tell him about her Gram, I notice Jasper's head goes back and he stares at the ceiling like he's begging for patience, so I stop talking.

"Get the FUCK out of here," he finally says. "After all the shit that went down with the Spiders, now we're short nearly ten grand and you come in here wanting to claim fucking Maddock's daughter as your goddamn Ol' Lady?" Slamming his hand on the desk when I try to speak, "Don't say a motherfucking word right now or I will fucking ban her ass from the clubhouse," Jasper seethes.

I sit back in my seat, keeping eye contact. Jasper and I have always been close, even more so since I handled Emma's ex-husband, so his goddamned threat pisses me off.

Flint enters the room without knocking. "Got your message, what's happening?" He starts before taking in the angry looks on both our faces. Then he pats me on the back in greeting and sits beside me. "Bree told me she met your girl the other night. She thinks you'll do well together."

Jasper pushes back from the desk, leaning over it.

"Yeah, let's start with that, Flint," he bites out. "Did Bree happen to mention that the girl's father is the Special Attorney investigating our asses? That the parts of this town the MC doesn't own, her family does? Because I am not fucking amused right now."

Flint's jaw drops open and he stares at me like he's never seen me before.

"Fuck. Gunner." I've always looked towards Flint as a father figure, but even he looks like he wants to skin me right now. "Tell me you didn't knock her up. Tell me you aren't that stupid."

"Can I talk?" I ask, lifting an eyebrow in Jasper's direction. With his nod, I continue. "My Riley isn't pregnant and her Gram knows about us. I've known Eileen Riley since I was a child and went to her to ask for fucking permission to be with her granddaughter nearly a year ago. I had to wait until she turned eighteen," I pause while Flint and Jas start swearing again. Louder and getting more pissed by the minute, I carry on.

"She's smart, in her second year at the university already. She's not close to her parents and moving into her own place this week. Her Gram actually set up a way to help her become independent of them. And I trust her. I trust her with my life."

Jas leans across the desk, "Just so we're crystal. Fucking. Clear on this one point. You didn't lay a goddamn finger on her before she turned eighteen, did you?"

"Fuck you for asking me that!" I snarl, lunging towards him before Flint gets between us.

Flint glares us back to our seats. "Jasper, you and I both know Gunner wouldn't do that." He sighs, running his hand over his face. "This is a whole new world of trouble, Gunner. Shitty relationship with her parents or not, when they find out you're banging their princess, they WILL come after us harder. All of us."

I sit silently, refusing to mention that we haven't actually had sex yet. Suddenly worried they'd order me away from her if they knew. "I've been loyal to the MC since the day I walked in. I've never asked for anything." I keep my tone even and sit looking back and forth between them. "I need her."

Jasper exhales. "Let's table this for now." Looking between Flint and me, he smirks and says, "The next issue doesn't seem so bad anymore."

Then he fills Flint and me in on what he has found, what he's done to try to track it and gets Flint on board to audit the numbers. Handing me a list of Brothers to look into and ordering us not to discuss either topic outside the room, he points to the door.

Flint claps me on the back again, asking me to stay for a drink. Knowing it wasn't really a question, I head to the bar with him. Getting straight to the point, he leads with, "You know, she wouldn't be the first girl who ran after the bad boy to get back at her parents, that's what it was with my ex. You sure she's worth it?"

"I'm sure," I order a draft from the probie behind the bar and drink half of it before turning back to Flint. "I've talked myself in and out of this relationship a hundred times since I met her. The one thing I know is that it's real. For both of us."

"No one mentioned Frank getting a swing in at you, so where'd you get your shiner?" Flint asks, probably trying for a safer subject. I accept a smoke from the probie and light up, fingering the lighter Riley sent me for Christmas.

"She's too fucking good for the likes of me, Man. I tried quitting her last night, stopping this, and she got a little pissed at me. Then we made up." I smile over at him, enjoying the rush of nicotine through my system.

Flint starts laughing until he sees my face, then turning my head to inspect the bruise, he whistles. "You're not shitting me, are you?"

Grinning at him, I shake my head. Making him laugh harder as he finishes his drink and orders another. "Huh. Princess or not, I think I may like her."

Vice comes out from the hall leading to the rooms, "Hey Gunner! Girlies are chattering about you. Any of that shit true?"

"Leave it alone, Vice, everyone knows I got a bigger dick than you," I shoot back at him.

"That'll be the day." He comes up to the bar and motions for a beer. "What is it with all you assholes settling down?"

I nod at him. Remembering something key, I set a reminder in my phone to order a 'Property of Gunner' cut for her when I leave here. Fucking gonna keep her wrapped up in that whenever she leaves the house.

"Well, better you than me, man." I smile at his sympathetic tone, he has no idea how lucky I got. "Bring her by when you're back, we'll tell her how great you are." Shit, my face goes pale at the thought.

CHAPTER THIRTEEN

GUNNER

I text her as I head out a short time later, heading to pick her up at the library and off on the dreaded shopping trip. I had never thought about how much stuff you need for an apartment but she wasn't kidding about filling two carts. It was actually four. With the back seats down, the worker I tipped to help us was barely able to stuff everything in my Explorer.

Before pulling out of the lot, I called a probie to meet us at her apartment to help unload. Arriving there, I send her up to organize everything that we unpacked then he and I take off for my shop. I wanted to get her the coffee table that she liked so much.

"That your woman, Gunner?" Probie works up the courage to ask on the drive across town. I nod, not saying anything. "She's real sweet." I nod again, trying to discourage this line of talk.

"That one Girlie? Uh, Deb, maybe? As soon as she showed up today, Betsy told her you said you were taken now. Deb totally lost her shit and slapped her. Fucking hard, man. Vice sent Deb home, told her to stay away a few days."

"Want to know some of the best advice I ever got?" Not caring that he nods, I continue. "Keep it wrapped up tight and don't go to any of the Girlies regularly. That last bit should have been, push away the Girlies that come to you too often. Thought it was convenient not having to signal for any of them. Never told Deb shit and stopped touching her when she started telling the others I was going to be hers."

"You know, I'm staying at my aunt's place for now. It's not far from Riley, want me to keep an eye on her when you're gone?" He offers, trying to win points with me.

"Nah, I got that handled. Just keep your mouth shut about where she lives, or you'll never get Patched."

"I won't say anything, not to anyone," the probie promises.

RILEY

I cannot believe how much I bought! I actually used the credit card my parents gave me instead of my savings. After Gunner left with the newest probie, I dug into organizing things and washing the sheets and towels I bought. When he realized I was picking out sheets, Gunner confessed to my housewarming gift, so I bought a few sets in the California King size.

After that, I couldn't stop smiling. He bought us a bed, just ours and with plenty of space to accommodate his size. Hearing a clammer on the steps, I open the door to see Probie and Gunner lugging the coffee table up the stairs.

They manage to get it in without destroying any of the drywall, then I go about showing Probie all the semi-secret compartments it has. He probably thinks I'm demented, but

I love it. Gunner looks on, pleased with my reaction, until he basically shoves Probie out of the apartment.

"Are you about done here?" He frowns at the disaster of tags and other items around us, but with things in the dryer, I'm actually at a good stopping point.

"We'll head to the cabin then, in the morning I will get you back to your SUV. I just need to be with you now." He sounds exhausted, so I quickly gather my things and follow him out.

Back at the cabin, I throw together a pasta dish and salad. He pulls me away from the table so we can eat next to each other on the sofa. Then tells me about Jasper and Flint's reactions to news about us. I absolutely lose my appetite. It had never occurred to me that his Brothers would, or could, order us apart. He explains about letting them think we've had sex and I smile, hoping that will push up whatever this crazy timeline is that he has in his head.

Afterwards, he straightens up the kitchen and we lie on the couch talking about everything and nothing. Gunner starts fingering my clit so softly at first I hardly notice it. Before long, I am straddling his lap and rubbing myself along his finger.

He sits back, almost lazily, watching me work for my own orgasm at his hands. Occasionally, he tweaks one of my nipples but mostly, his other hand is cupping my cheek to maintain our eye contact.

"Please, Gunner!" I yell as I get close to coming. He pinches my clit causing me to scream, then he swiftly rubs my clit with his soaked finger until I explode. I collapse against his chest and he quickly shifts me, cradling me in his arms until I drift off.

Waking up early the next morning, I'm warm from his body heat and having most of my clothes from yesterday on.

He had stripped down to his boxers before getting us into bed, so grinning up at his snoring form I quickly decide on a little surprise and move down towards the center of the bed.

His penis roars to life when I touch it. Taking it into my mouth and feeling it grow as I suck on it is really encouraging, but I love the gasp he lets out as he wakes up. "Dammit Riley, that's Fucking IT." He gets out before threading his fingers through my hair as my mouth moves up and down his rod.

Gunner's length quickly exceeds what I can hold in my mouth, and though I try to take more of it in, I can't stop the resulting gag. Pulling my head back, he puts one hand on the base of his cock, stopping my further attempts at deep throating him.

"Another time, Sweetheart. Just keep going."

As the big guy requests, I continue, focusing on the sensitive areas I found the first time I did this and a few minutes later I'm rewarded for my efforts. He once again grunts out a warning, but the first shot of cum hitting the back of my throat still surprises me and I have a hard time swallowing it all down without dripping any.

Finishing up by swirling my tongue around his now softening cock, I lean in to kiss its head and quickly lick up the last of his seed that keeps bubbling up from the tip.

As I crawl up the bed, he hooks his hands under my arms to pull me up and firmly plants his mouth on mine. I am surprised he has no problem kissing me when I just had his cum in my mouth but his touch quickly erases all thoughts.

"Wake me up anytime you want, Sweetheart," he murmurs against my mouth, biting my lower lip. Pulling back from our kiss, he folds me into his body.

“I’m looking forward to practicing more—on you—though!” After last time, I thought it important to clarify.

“What time does your class start?” Gunner whispers into my hair.

“Not until 10:15. “

“Let’s get going, I’ll take you to your SUV then get to Mrs. R’s place. Uh, can I get a key to your apartment to meet the delivery team for the mattress?”

“Shit! I forgot you were seeing Gram today. What are you going to talk about?” I’m debating skipping my database class to tag along.

Tapping me on the nose, Gunner laughs, “You’re going to class. She and I have a lot to cover. I’ll fill you in later.”

GUNNER

With Riley off, I head to Mrs. R’s a full thirty minutes early. Unperturbed, her butler/chauffeur/right-hand man, Rogers, brings me right in to see her.

“Good Morning, Alex! I thought you’d be early today.” Of course, she did, I think, flinching at the sound of my given name.

“Mrs. R, you know how I feel about you, but I’d like to know what you’ve got up that sleeve of yours. No more games.” I stare down at her.

“Have a seat, Alex; I’ll develop a crick in my neck otherwise.” Sighing, I do as she asks.

“What happened to your eye?” She asks, leaning forward.

“Riley,” I grunt.

“Did you deserve it?”

“Yes.”

“You didn’t betray her, I trust?”

"With that temper, I'm pretty sure she'd geld me if I had." Mrs. R sits patiently until I elaborate. "I don't deserve her, I want her more than anything but she's so goddamn..."

"Language, Alex!"

"Sorry. She's so, just, everything. I tried to walk away the other night, give her an out. Then I tried to touch her and she knocked the sh...sorry, um, she gave me the smackdown I deserved for hurting her."

"You're acting like a schoolboy, Alex. I trust you with her, now you need to trust yourself." She raises an eyebrow at me and I feel like I've been hit again.

"I told Jasper and Flint."

She giggles. "And how did that go over, Dear?"

Frowning at her, "About like you'd expect. I would hazard a guess that you've been making plans for her this past year. Care to let me in on them?"

"I'm not getting any younger. I will make sure she's taken care of and I know enough about her miscreant parents to be able to protect you. With the obvious caveats."

"Riley is safe and happy." I fill in the blank and she nods imperiously.

"Don't think being with her will be a free ride, though, Alex. I won't make the same mistake I did with her mother."

"Mrs. R, I don't want your money nor any of hers. I make enough to support us, not to the level she's had but she'll know she's loved. Every day, she'll know that. I swear."

"Very good, Alex. Have you told her?" I duck my head, looking away.

"No, I mean, we've only had a few days together."

"I expect you to do so before making use of that huge bed you bought!" My jaw drops, and she gives me that little grin of hers. That same grin that frustrates Riley, because there's a world of machinations behind it. "The one caveat you didn't guess, Alex. Any children she has must be college educated, I insist on it even if they chose to follow you into the Grizzlies. I will leave money for that and any medical issues that may arise, but do not expect a golden goose."

"That's more than generous, but just so you know any children we have will attend the local school. None of that private tutor bull..., well, and I also hope you will agree that if not college, then a technical institute of some sort?"

"Acceptable," Mrs. R smiles and nods to herself. "You realize you just advocated harder for possible future children than Riley's parents ever did for her? Do stop thinking you aren't just what Riley needs most. Now, this certainly hasn't been our usual chat nor can I offer you lunch today. I had to schedule another appointment. You needn't wait a month, if you wish to visit sooner, Dear."

Crossing over to her, I ignore the surprised look on her face as I drop a kiss on her cheek. "Take care of yourself, Gram." I wink at her before heading out, enjoying her laugh as I close her parlor door.

EILEEN RILEY

Seeing Alex, or Gunner, as he prefers, all grown up makes me feel old. He was such a solemn boy, and as he grew his grandmother would talk of his honesty and loyalty. Even if he got himself in trouble he wouldn't lie.

Ava was a good woman with an oaf for a son. As disgraceful as Alex's start in life was, she always did right by him. In the years since his return from the Marines, I have been pleasantly surprised that he has kept up with our visits, giving me plenty of notice if another commitment arose or staying around to help fix something he sees around here.

I am not blind to his antics. I had him investigated when his visits became a regular fixture, trying to figure out if he was looking to get something from me. He never asked for a thing, instead, he would bring pastries from the bakery and even gifted me a beautiful side table one Christmas. While he never discusses anything about the MC, other than an occasional mention of Flint, in this house, I have been pleased with his plans for his furniture business.

Then came the day he did ask for something. The most precious thing in the world to me.

Initially, the thought of this rough, dour, giant of a biker with my kind, happy granddaughter, who is well over a foot shorter than him, shocked me. As he spoke, I started to picture the serious, earnest child, rather than the man before me and realized he could be the best chance for Riley to find happiness. While I initially gave him my blessing, it wasn't until I next saw Riley that I was convinced. The girl was glowing.

Riley did not have a conventional childhood, hers was lonely and she turned to books for companions very early on. Because of this, she is wise beyond her years and, due to her parents, she does not trust people easily.

I began to make plans for Riley and Gunner. I knew she had no interest in pre-med, but that would be up to her to work out. However, she would need a decent place to live and an income. I could provide that for her, as long as she pitched in with becoming a responsible property manager/owner. Next would be the issue between my son-in-law's position in State politics and Gunner's position in the MC. Well, I could handle that also.

Appearances are deceiving, and Riley's parents have become quite the shady characters over the years. I sat back and watched, collecting information from my investigator.

Releasing that is not in my best interest, but the knowledge of it could smooth any kick-up the MC leadership would foresee.

FLINT

Double Double Toil and Trouble.

Being called to Mrs. Riley's home was hardly how I expected this day to go. I knew her husband a bit; he was older than me but we'd had some dealings. Nowadays most of the commercial property in town is divided up between the MC and Mrs. Riley.

She's always been one to hold things close to the vest; I would not like to play poker with her at all. The old Shakespeare/Macbeth line has always sounded in my head when I've been around her, and today is no different. Though I hardly need a crystal ball to know what the topic will be.

Fucking Gunner. With the deals we have lined up the last thing any of us needs is Maddock coming after us harder and that goddamn giant makes a move to abscond with the man's teenage daughter. I love Gunner like a son, but that is some serious bullshit to bring our way.

Pulling up in front of Mrs. Riley's home, I brace myself for this conversation.

"Flint! I'm so glad you weren't early," she calls out as I'm shown in to see her.

"You are looking lovely, as always." Eileen Riley was a renowned beauty in her day and the years have been kind to her. I have never seen her granddaughter but can't imagine her being anything but beautiful.

"I understand you are to be married?" I nod in reply, sitting across from her. "I would like to meet this woman.

She bought the bar property from under our noses, I understand?"

"Yes, she pretty much runs it with Rusty now. Great lady," I concede.

"Well, she brought you to heel, so I would expect so." I raise my eyebrow at Mrs. Riley's comment; trying real hard to respect my elders.

"I understand your granddaughter has brought Gunner to heel. No mean feat there." I tilt my head to the side, she's not that much older than me, after all.

"Well done, Flint." She benevolently smiles at me. "My husband always did enjoy your company. Which brings us to your visit." I lean back and let her speak.

Thirty minutes later, my head is spinning as I'm standing on her doorstep. I have to get to Jasper. I have to let him know I've agreed to validate Gunner's claim on Riley when he formally makes it. That and Mrs. Riley's assurances she will tie her son-in-law's hands in the event of any interference from his side.

Double Double Toil and Trouble, indeed.

That woman is diabolical. Again, I can't help but wonder what her granddaughter is like. I shudder at the thought of either of them and my Bree ganging up.

CHAPTER FOURTEEN

RILEY

Classes are going really well this term, liking the subject matter puts school in a whole new light for me. My three classes and time in the lab speed by and before long I'm texting Gunner that I'm heading to the apartment. Checking my missed calls, I see that I have two from my mom and a text that it's urgent to call her.

Sitting in my SUV, I decide it's safer to get this out of the way before hitting the road and silently hoping that they will be asleep as they're eight hours ahead of me right now.

"Riley." She picks up on the first ring. "Where have you been?"

Frowning at the phone, I reply, "Class."

"Your tone is inappropriate, and you know what I mean, young lady. I checked the logs for the home security system and you have barely been there plus I see a large charge on a card you barely ever use. At the Superstore, no less."

"I am in the process of moving out actually. Gram gave

me a place in town," I reply, trying to act my age and not beat around the bush.

"Absolutely not, Riley. We will discuss this when your father and I get back. We expect you to concentrate on your schoolwork, then you can move away for med school but not undergrad while we're footing your bills."

"I expected to have this conversation when you returned. I am no longer in pre-med. I was able to secure a scholarship for a CIS degree."

"That is not acceptable. I will be calling the school next. You will be changed back to the right track immediately." Mother is snarling at me. I understand this is a lot to take in, but I always told them what I wanted.

"Mom, I actually turned eighteen this past weekend." I sigh into the phone. "This is my decision now, I am happy to further explain my plans with you and Father upon your return, but staying at home or returning to pre-med is out of the question. I wanted to discuss this with you after New Year's, but you and Father ended up going to D.C. without letting me know."

"Riley, I don't think YOU understand. All of our friends are aware of your future path. This is not to be borne." Her voice has gotten shrill and I can hear my father start to make noises in the background.

"I'm sure it's late there. Let's speak when you are better rested." I silently disconnect. Wiping the tears that are streaming down my cheeks, I start back to town. God forbid I let down their friends' expectations.

Nearly to my apartment, my phone rings. Seeing a number from my school advisor, I sigh and pick up. "Mr. Elwood, how are you?"

He snorts at me. "Been better. The president of the university just spent ten minutes yelling then hung up on me. It seems I was supposed to notify your parents of your degree change."

"I know I was seventeen when I applied for the change, but I am eighteen now so it is my decision." I brace myself for the fallout.

"Relax, Miss Maddock. You see, that is where you are correct. You are legally responsible for yourself now. And, as I reminded our esteemed president, the university is in the business of guiding children to become adults. Keep your grades up and your head on straight, all right?"

"Yes, sir, and I am sorry you've been put in this position." Phew. We say our goodbyes and disconnect as I'm pulling up to the apartment, right behind Gunner's Explorer.

I head inside my nearly empty place and call out to him. "Back here!" Comes the reply. I walk towards the master bedroom to see him making the bed.

"I hoped to get this set up before you got home, Sweetheart," Gunner crosses towards me, distracting me from a huge, nearly-made mattress sitting atop an amazing dark wood platform with a padded headboard. "Took me longer than I thought to get the platform reassembled up here."

I look between Gunner and the bed. "Gunner! It's beautiful! You are amazing!" I wrap myself around his midsection and hold him tightly to me, squealing as he suddenly picks me up and tosses me in the center of the bed.

"Had to test it!" He laughs down at me, quickly joining me, he covers my face with kisses. "I wanted it to be perfect for you, and we can change out the platform if you don't like it."

I stop him with my finger over his lips, smiling up at him. "I love it. I may need a ladder to get into bed though!"

He is so much taller than me that I don't think he accounted for the height with the mattress on top of it.

"Outta bed, Sweetheart, or we'll be here till morning!" He rolls me to my side to give my ass a quick swat before sliding off the bed. Groaning, I follow him slowly, preferring to stay in bed.

"I didn't eat much today and wanted to take you out, okay?" He asks.

I quickly nod and go searching for towels. Showering and getting ready, I walk out to the living room to find him pacing. "Everything alright, Gunner?" I pause, tensing up.

He spins to face me then freezes.

"You're so beautiful, Riley," he says in his smoke-roughened voice. Crossing to me he kisses me until all the stress of the past couple hours evaporates. Smiling at him as he reaches for my jacket. "Come on, if we stay here you'll starve."

Going downstairs in silence, I see our trucks lightly coated in snow, dim streetlights reflecting off of them. "Where to, Big Guy?" I ask, tugging on his hand and trying to keep up with his long pace.

"I could use a steak," he slows down, then opens the passenger side of his Explorer and deposits me inside.

We drive across town, avoiding the tourist options and park outside the local favorite. Walking inside, I notice Gunner once again scans all available seats and selects one to his liking. The host hurries to catch up to us. This time, Gunner sits next to me in the booth and sends the host away with our drink order.

"I don't think I'll be back before Saturday, you okay with that?" He starts, and I'm quiet not expecting his sudden launch into this topic. "The weather looks like shit and I don't want to push it," Gunner continues.

"Thanks for letting me know, just text if you're able." I can't control this aspect of his life and won't attempt to try right now. "I just have classes, homework, and then I will see Gram on Friday night. Oh, I have to start finding someone to rent the store also."

"Can you give me a week or so on that? I have an idea. I'll run it by you when I think it through more. Maybe when I'm back?" I nod, glad to put this off for a little bit. The waiter stops by for our order, both he and Gunner give me incredulous looks as I order the chili, an eight-ounce filet, garlic mashed potatoes, and sautéed spinach. Puh-lease, I barely ate earlier.

"So, my mother reached out to me today," I start. He pauses, having started to lean into my neck. "She'd seen the charge on the credit card then checked the security logs for the house. I had to tell her everything, well, not everything. I didn't mention you. Not yet."

"I bet everything else went over like a ton of bricks." He wraps his arm tighter around me while swirling the condensation around the outside of his beer mug with his other hand.

"I told her about the apartment, didn't mention the storefront. Then I brought up my change in major, pointing out that I had been telling them I wanted to do it. Her biggest argument was that it would look bad to their friends who have heard about my future plans. Can you believe that?" I reach out for his beer mug, but seeing the waiter approach with my chili, I draw my hand back and down nearly all of my Coke. Gunner asks for another beer. "Right before I got home my advisor called me. Mom had already called the freaking president of the university trying to get my decision reversed. Then the president gave my advisor an earful!"

The waiter arrives with the beer and Gunner asks for another, the waiter gives me major side-eye, knowing the reason for all the beers.

"I saw your Gram today," he says as I'd forgotten he was heading there earlier. He slides the newly arrived beer in front of me while I start in on the chili. "As we thought, she seems to have spent the last eight months figuring out the details. She didn't share much but said to leave it to her." Swallowing, he gets quiet for a moment.

"She really doesn't like them, does she?" He asks me quietly.

"My parents?" At his nod, I continue, "they never spend any time together, I don't know if they speak." I shrug. "Hey, she likes us!" I laugh up at him as the food arrives. Then I'm too busy eating to speak much.

Leaning back with a groan after he cleans the meat off the bone of his steak, "I love that you eat like a real person, Riley." I can only smile, as I finish up my spinach. "I love you period."

I freeze. He said it so softly I wonder if I didn't just have a hallucination. A moment ticks by in silence.

"You can take it back. Food coma rules?" I close my mouth to stop myself from babbling.

"Not taking it back. Probably won't say it much. Sorry, Sweetheart, but you gotta know that I do."

Shaking and pushing him out of the booth, afraid to make eye contact, I say, "Get the check, Gunner. Now, please." Pulling my jacket on, I head towards the door leaving a dumbfounded behemoth in my wake.

I wait at the door then as he nears I head out into the cold night air; approaching the passenger side of his truck, he looks wary as he asks, "What are we doing, Sweetheart?"

Facing the truck door, I speak up, "You're taking me

home and making me yours, Gunner. No more waiting." I'm scooped up and deposited in the truck before I can breathe properly.

After he parks in front of the apartment, I wait for him to open the door. He carries me straight from the seat up to the master bedroom like my weight is insignificant.

I start stripping the moment he sets me down. Noticing he hasn't moved, I crawl up to the center of the bed. Kneeling on the middle of it, I face him and say, "I love you, too."

GUNNER

I can barely see her in the darkness but have already memorized her curves. Each time I saw her, I thought that might be the last. Telling her I loved her started a storm in my chest, it would not be calmed until we reached the room and she did exactly what I needed her to do without being prompted.

Not saying a word, not breaking eye contact, I take my turn removing my clothes. Reaching into my back pocket for a condom, she holds up her hand. "Not tonight, Gunner. Tomorrow we'll be responsible adults. Tonight I want to feel your skin on mine, no matter what comes of it."

I gulp. I've never been bare in a woman before. I open my mouth to object, and then stop myself. Because, no matter what she sees in me, as I've always known, I am a selfish bastard and do not see a downside to getting her pregnant nor marking her with my cum.

Without a word, I move, naked, onto the bed next to her. As she sways into me I shake my head, instead, reaching my hands out and pinching each of her nipples tightly between my index fingers and thumbs.

"Who do you belong to?" I ask her harshly.

"You, only you, Gunner," she moans, arching towards me.

"Show me how wet you are, Sweetheart," I command, enjoying the widening of her eyes. Then with a downward glance, she shifts her right hand across her thigh and delves it into her pussy, taking her time in there. Looking back at me, her hips arching towards my hard cock she pulls out her first two fingers, I grab her wrist and move her hand to circle my cock. Wrapping her fingers around me and spreading her moisture up and down my length until I can't take anymore.

I push her onto her back, spreading her thighs wide apart, I duck my face between them. Dipping my tongue into her core and I swirl her juices around the lips of her pussy and up to her clit. Nipping her clit gently between my teeth, I suck it further into my mouth, circling it with my tongue.

Pressing first one then a second finger into her hot, wet center, I slowly work on preparing her body for my cock. I know there will be pain regardless but will do what I can to ease that. Lifting my mouth, I tell her to play with her nipples. She moans before complying, staring into my eyes, her own, half-hooded with pleasure. I long to slide a finger into her asshole but decide to wait for another time. Her orgasm is all but on top of her and I want her to come before I sink my dick into her.

Her moaning increases as she moves a hand down, weaving her fingers into my hair. "Please, Gunner?! I need it." She starts begging, so I go to town on her clit and in a moment her thighs start squeezing on either side of my head and her core lifts off the bed as she screams my name repeatedly, squirting all over me.

As she relaxes back against the bed, I move up along her body pausing to lick each nipple, I reach for her chin and wait for her eyes to focus on mine. "Ready for me, Sweetheart? I got to have you now."

Her mouth widens into a small smile as she simultaneously spreads her thighs and lifts her hips, so her wet pussy rubs up against my cock.

"You'll be mine now, Gunner?" Riley whispers.

"Yes, Riley, just yours." I don't think I've ever spoken truer words. Moving on top of her, I nudge my cock into her folds just to moisten the head. We both groan at the same time. I am shaking with need as she raises her hand to my cheek and nods.

I plunge into her, breaking past her barrier until I'm fully buried inside my Sweetheart.

Riley's eyes widen with surprise as a brief shadow of pain passes through them. I stay still, barely breathing, hoping she's alright. Riley takes a deep breath then subconsciously squeezes my cock even tighter within her. I've never felt the like. She's impossibly tight, wonderfully warm and wet and it takes every bit of control I have not to come right now.

"Riley?" I won't move without permission.

Tilting her hips even further up, she bestows a larger smile on me. "More, Gunner. I need more." Leaning down to distract her with a kiss her as I withdraw, she moans at the loss and wraps her legs around my hips to encourage me quickly back. "More, Gunner? Please, all of it."

She doesn't ask for much.

I start to slowly thrust in and out of her, but she senses I am holding back and continues begging me for more. Soon I'm pounding into her. My full length into her virgin slit, supporting my weight on one arm, reaching down to rub her clit wanting her to come hard, squeezing my dick for all she's worth.

"Come with me, Riley. I need you to come with me," I moan barely able to hold back.

"Come inside me, Gunner! I want to feel it. I'm going to..." Riley is bucking underneath me, barely able to speak. Finally, she grabs my shoulders, nails sinking into my flesh, and screams loudly into the night. Her tight sheath strangles the cum from my cock and my cries drown out hers as I pour myself into her, filling her with my seed.

My cock slowly softens and I roll to my side, taking her with me. Squeezing too tightly, I let up when she pokes me in the chest. Dropping a kiss to her temple, I whisper how perfect she is, needing her to know I've never felt this way. Feeling her tears on my chest and hearing a soft sob, I'm filled with panic. Pulling back to see her face, I'm terrified I've hurt her.

CHAPTER FIFTEEN

GUNNER

"What is it, Sweetheart? What did I do?" I cup her face in my as she wipes her tears with her hands and drawing herself back into my chest.

Her voice is muffled and broken from crying, but I manage to make out "perfect" and "love you" so I adjust my hold around her, soothing her and lightly kissing her head. As my heartbeat returns to normal, I roll off the bed; knowing I need to tend to her. Shushing her question, I pad to the bathroom and after quickly rinsing her blood and juices off my dick, I return with a partially wet towel and a spare.

"Here, Sweetheart, lay back." I direct her, moving between her legs I gently wipe away our mixed creams and a smear of blood. I freeze, transfixed, as more of my cum slips from her body, my cock twitches again. So fucking hot knowing that there's more of me inside her even now.

"There you go, Riley," I say, dropping a quick kiss down

to the narrow tuft of hair between her thighs. I shift her to a drier area of the bed, placing the other towel under her ass and covering us as I lay back beside her.

RILEY

I've never felt so treasured in my life.

I knew from the day we met this is how he would treat me if I were his.

"I love you, Gunner," I murmur as I drift off to sleep.

Early the next morning I awake to a softly snoring Gunner and the distant chirping of my phone. Disentangling myself, I grab his shirt as I walk to the front room to retrieve my phone from the purse I dropped near the door. Three missed calls from Gram, this can't be good.

"Good Morning, Riley," she answers on the first ring. "I trust you are well?"

"Yes, Gram. I saw you've been calling, is everything alright?" I ask while grabbing a Diet Coke from the fridge.

"Well, I had an interesting call this morning. Officer Kennelly, you know that busybody?" She pauses for acknowledgement.

"Yes, Gram? What happened?" I can't imagine anything good coming from a call from him. He gives me the creeps.

"Well, it seems your parents have occasionally tasked him with keeping an eye out for you when they're gone. Last night he was at the same restaurant as you and Alex..."

"Alex?"

"Gunner, Dear. Do keep up." I suddenly feel like an idiot

for not realizing Gunner wasn't his given name. "He said he left a voicemail for your parents about you being in inappropriate company, then drove by the house this morning and saw that no one was home. Unable to reach them, he called me to see if you were with me."

"Of all the nerve! How dare he go running around checking up on me!" I can't help but yell, Gunner is instantly in the doorway of the bedroom looking concerned. "I haven't had the chance to tell you, but Mother called to check up on me yesterday. She knows about me changing my major and the apartment. She forbade both decisions, and even called the president of the university trying to get him to get me reassigned to pre-med."

"Well, we can expect they've heard about you and Alex now also." She sighs into the phone. "I suppose they'll shorten their trip. I know you can handle this, just be firm with them. I wanted to let you know. You be sure to call me if they give you any problems. Give Alex my regards, Dear."

Standing, in the living room, I'm staring at the phone as a still naked Gunner wraps his arms around me. "What's going on?"

"Officer Kennelly left a voicemail for my parents that he saw us out together. Then after driving by their house and not seeing anyone home he called my Gram 'concerned about my well-being.' Gram thinks my parents will come home early," I explain.

He has tensed up around me. "Shit, are you going to be alright? I can't cancel my trip."

"I know, I'll be fine. I have class the next few days, then you'll be back again." With my arms around his back, I look up at the concerned expression on his face, before I grab his ass with both hands. "Follow me if you'd like a proper send-off!" I try to move out of his hold but he bends down to toss me over his shoulder instead.

Laughing, I scream, "Caveman!" Getting a growl in return. As he steps over the jeans he discarded the night before and I remember the condom. Deciding not to further push our luck, I ask Gunner to get it.

After placing me on the bed, he retrieves it. "Sweetheart, last night was my first time without one of these. Maybe after you're on the pill a while, we can talk about me going bare again?" He looks sheepish at making the request.

I grin and nod, not looking forward to having a barrier between us.

"First things first! I want to try doggie style, Gunner." He lunges at me, smothering me with his weight as he kisses my nipples and mouth. Finally leaning back, he unwraps the condom to wrap himself up. "On your hands and knees, Riley. Now!"

I quickly comply but still get spanked for my efforts. Screaming in surprise, I lean my ass back into his palm as he soothes the area. "Spread your thighs a bit more. That's good." He slides a finger inside me, moaning as he feels how wet I am. "That's my good girl, all ready for me. Tell me what you want, Sweetheart."

"You, Gunner. Please!" I moan, thrusting myself back on his finger.

He spanks me again, "Tell me exactly what you want."

"Your cock, Gunner!" I pant, the one finger he's holding out, letting me fuck myself with, is not nearly enough.

Another spank. "Where, Sweetheart?"

Nearly sobbing with need as he withdraws his finger, I beg, "I need your cock in my pussy, Gunner. I need your cock in me, so bad."

Kneeling behind me, he slowly enters my overheated pussy. "You're so tight. Squeezing me so hard." He keeps narrating as he gradually sheaths his full length.

With one hand on my hip and the other on my shoulder, he stays inside me, gyrating his hips and driving me crazy. "Fuck me, Gunner, please don't tease me. I need it hard." From this position, I can feel him so much deeper than last night but he's still holding back.

Reaching to grab both my tits in his hands, he starts pounding into me. "That's it, talk dirty, Riley. Show me what a dirty little girl you are for my cock. This is what you'll get." I lose all capacity to think.

"Yes, fuck me. Fuck me as hard as you want!" He pinches my nipples and I see stars. It's like there's a live wire connected between my nipples and my pussy and it pushes me right over the edge. His hands slide down to my hips as he continues to thrust through my orgasm until he reaches his own.

I am lost. And found. The moments he is away disposing of the condom seem like an eternity. Then I'm pulled back into his chest.

"I'll always give you what you need, Sweetheart, but you damn well better get used to asking for it." He whispers into my ear as he gently flicks it with his tongue. "I'm going to miss you, Ri. I'll get back to you as soon as I can."

"Just be safe, Gunner, that's all that matters to me." I push aside dark 'what if' thoughts. We lie awake, just content to be in each other's arms.

Before long, Gunner is kissing me goodbye and heading out to start his run. Although I have time before class, there's too much running through my mind for me to sleep. That's when I decide to go for some retail therapy. I need some furniture after all!

Ninety minutes later, I'm at a mid-range furniture store and select a sofa and an oversized chair with a matching ottoman. Not wanting to spend much of my own reserves, I decide the second bedroom can stay empty for the foreseeable future and after arranging delivery I head to class.

CHAPTER SIXTEEN

GUNNER

Getting to the clubhouse, I first head to my room, taking a mental inventory of what is mine versus what was here when I moved in. Riley and I haven't discussed moving in together, not like there's been time. I'm hoping that she'll want me there with her and I'm not pushing my luck. I go through my clothes, packing what I'll need for the next few days then a weekend at Riley's.

Heading back to the office, I find it empty so drop my bag inside the door and head to the kitchen. Betsy is in there with another of the Girlies, cooking for Flint, Connal, Jake, Vice, and Royce. I fix a coffee and nod to her when asked if I'm hungry.

Shooting the shit with the guys calms me down. I've been running high on Riley's presence for days. Knowing better than to discuss our business in front of the Girlies, they catch me up on the goings on and rib me about being pussy whipped. I have no problem with that and take their shit easily, surprised when Royce speaks up in defense of my new status.

"Vice, have you even seen her? She's fucking hot as shit. Can't figure out what she's doing with Ugly over here, cause I know I would have given up all this free and easy," Royce waves his hand around, "to get with her." I narrow my eyes at him but decide to stick with the food in front of me rather than smacking him.

I also don't miss the stiffening of the Girlies backs at his reference to their status with the MC, once again showing that Royce has to learn to muzzle himself. Meanwhile, Vice and Flint share a look, knowing who Riley's family is.

As the others move on, Connal, Flint, and I are left in the kitchen. "Guys, I, well, I gave Riley both of your numbers. Apparently, Kennelly saw us out the other night and told her parents. They've been traveling but may be on their way back now. I know she can count on her grandmother, but I'll text you her new address and maybe you can check in on her?"

Connal sits back in his seat, studying me closely. "What am I missing here? Why would Kennelly know her or get involved?"

Before I can respond, Flint speaks up. "Keep it close for now. She's the Maddocks' daughter."

"Da Fuck, Gunner!" Connal can't contain his surprise. "Did you know that day you brought her to my garage?"

"No, not until that bit about her allowance. I knew her mother's maiden name was Riley, so I put it together then."

"Shit, Brother. This isn't good. How do you see this thing going?" He pours himself more coffee but looks at it like he'd like something harder.

"I'm going to claim her." He lets out a low whistle at my

response. "Meanwhile, I know I can trust you, you and Flint both. Will you do this for me?"

"Sure, maybe I'll meet the Governor while I'm at it!" He slaps me on the back and heads out shaking his head.

"I want to meet with her," Flint turns to me.

"Sure, I'll bring her by Bree's when I'm..."

"No." Flint brings his fist down on the table. "I'm gonna have Bree call her and let her know I'll be by tonight."

"Flint?"

"You want her, Gunner? I'll back it, but not until I take her measure. End of discussion. Now Jasper should be in his office, so go check in then be on your way."

Twenty minutes later, Royce, Vice, and I are on our way, split between two vehicles. Riding in cages during the winter months is necessary around these mountains especially when carrying product, but frustrating nonetheless. I'm in no mood for Royce's shit and it takes a while for him to settle down.

FLINT

Right as dusk is turning to night, I pull up in front of an empty storefront and follow the directions Bree gave me about Riley's door. She was right. The doorbell is a pain in the ass to make out from the brick surrounding it.

After I'm buzzed in and halfway up the stairs, the upper door opens and I finally see what all the fuss is about. Barefoot, in sweats, and her brown hair in a messy ponytail, is a pretty slip of a girl with extraordinary eyes.

My own Bree has these gorgeous hazel eyes that swirl and change with her mood. Riley's are amber, an eye color I've never seen before and they almost glow. Although not as beautiful as her grandmother was at her age, she is as easy to read as an open book and as both Bree and Gunner said, "there's just something about her that makes me want to protect her, to be a part of her life." I don't know what it is, or if this girl even needs protecting, but I suddenly find myself agreeing with their sentiment.

She's reaching her hand towards me and I realize I've stopped to stare at her. "Good to meet you, Flint. Come on in."

She grips my hand firmly and gives me a half smile, showing front teeth that slightly overlap. "I'm so sorry I can't offer you a seat! I do have coffee though?"

Looking around, there is nothing in the room but a coffee table and piles of books. "When did you move in?"

"Officially, yesterday after we came back from the cabin. Gunner is responsible for my two pieces of furniture, but I ordered a couch and chair today and would love to have you and Bree over for dinner soon. I'm a reasonably good cook." She timidly smiles up at me and I realize she's nervous about my visit.

I nod, I'll let Bree handle that. "You're smaller than I expected." I can just imagine what that other piece of furniture is.

"I get that a lot. My Gram and mother have like five inches on me," she snorts, waving a hand into the air.

I nod again, not even sure why I mentioned it. She hands me a cup of coffee, indicating sugar and milk.

Leaning against the counter, I start, "As you can guess, I'm trying to wrap my head around a Maddock throwing over her life for a biker."

She narrows her eyes at me and says, "He is more than that silly label, as I expect you know."

"But how do you? You've spent, what four days with him? What about the life you had? This life we lead, it affects those around us. Don't fucking kid yourself that it won't." I say slowly after taking a big gulp of coffee.

"What do you know about the life I had?" Red is creeping up her neck, but she isn't backing down. Well, I suppose if she can stand up to Gunner she won't back down from me either.

"Well, then, the life you could have?" I shrug, dismissing her anger. Thinking that the best way of protecting her might be to run her off.

"I've waited long enough to be out from under my parent's control. Before meeting Gunner, I had planned to transfer out of state. This way, I can still be a part of my Gram's life and in a region I love. With a man I love."

"What happens when he has one too many drinks one night and fucks some easy snatch?" I raise an eyebrow at her, just gauging her responses now.

"He won't." She looks ready to do battle.

RILEY

"Has Gunner ever broken his word to you?" I continue, wanting to smack this man. Letting the silence draw out, he finally shakes his head. "Then why do you think his word to me is worthless?"

"It's the life, Princess. One way or another, it gets to us all." Flint finishes his coffee. "I best be getting back to Bree. Think about it good and hard."

I watch him leave in silence. What can I say to this man who's known Gunner for so many years? I lock the door, hit the lights and wander back to the bedroom. Crawling into the space Gunner slept in last night, I will myself not to cry until I finally fall asleep.

CHAPTER SEVENTEEN

RILEY

THE NEXT DAY I'M ON AUTOPILOT. BREAKFAST, CLASSES, LUNCH then the library. Leaving later than I planned, I get to the parking lot, only to wander around in a circle. My SUV is gone. I dig out my phone to call campus security, only to notice a text from my mom telling me where to meet their driver when I'm ready to leave campus.

Fuck. They're back and they took back the car they bought me. Taking deep breaths, I head back to the warmth of the student center. I need to think. Their driver will only take me to their house. I'll be a virtual prisoner. I can call Flint or Connal, but that still leaves me without transportation in the coming days. Gram is my only option.

Fighting back tears, I dial her. No answer, so I try her cell. Straight to voicemail. I consider this a bit of an emergency, so I call her driver, Rogers.

Success! "Rogers! I'm so happy you answered."

"Of course, Miss Riley. Your grandmother is unavailable right now. May I assist you?"

"Please. Long story, but I no longer have a vehicle and I'm stranded on campus. Can you possibly come get me?" Silence stretches out so I'm forced to repeat his name, in case the call was dropped.

"Your parents are here, Miss Riley. From the volume of their voices, it seems unpleasant and I would prefer to stay nearby. Perhaps if you could take a taxi and I can meet you in town with the fare?"

"Is she alright?"

"Yes, Miss Riley. It's merely your parents. How about if I run over to your apartment and leave the money in an envelope inside the downstairs door?" He suggests.

"Thank you so much, Rogers! I will come by in the morning."

"Good evening, Miss Riley. I'll let your grandmother know to expect you."

Walking down to the security gate, I ask them to get a cab for me. While there are raised eyebrows, I'm shown a warm place to stay and before long I'm heading back to my apartment. Finding the money, as Rogers promised, I'm soon home. My own home, albeit an empty one.

Knowing I won't be able to reach Gunner and calling Gram this late, especially after any earlier upset she might have had, would be selfish, I hesitate a moment and call Bree.

Going straight to her voicemail, I decide to leave her one; more out of a need to speak than anything else. "Bree. It's Riley. You may be working late. I'm sorry, I shouldn't bother you, just wanted to hear a friendly voice. Um, no need to call back."

Feeling like an idiot, I decide to wait until the morning and text Connal, he may know of an inexpensive car I can buy. Making some hot chocolate and heading to bed, my phone rings.

"Riley, you ok, Hon?" I'm so relieved to hear Bree's voice, I almost start crying.

"Bree, I'm sorry, I shouldn't have..."

"No. I meant to call you earlier, Flint shouldn't have said what he did and I already gave him an earful."

"Oh, no, it's just I was at school and the library then I came out and my parents had taken my SUV. They left a driver behind for me but I ended up in a cab. I was scared they wouldn't let me out of the house. I'm sure I'm just being paranoid, but..." I can't stop babbling.

"Shit! Riley, are you at your apartment? Is anyone with you?" She asks, instantly concerned.

"I'm here alone."

"Can I bring my dog? I'll be there in twenty minutes." I'm so relieved to hear her suggest this but hate feeling so needy.

"I don't have any furniture, just a bed. And nothing for a dog to eat." I can't help my ragged breath right now.

"I'll be there soon. Don't you worry. We'll have a girls' night. I'll call you from outside so you know it's me."

True to her word, Bree is at my place twenty minutes later. A beautiful dog is bounding up the stairs ahead of her. "His name is Ragnar, ok if he just explores a bit?" I laugh, as Ragnar runs all around then circles back between us.

She comes in, dropping a duffle bag near the door and moves to place another bag on the kitchen counter. "This place is darling! Can I leave Ragnar's food up here? He'll get into it otherwise."

I nod and walk over to hug her. "Thank you for coming, I know you were busy. I didn't have anyone else to call right now."

“Shush! It was nothing. Now I said a girls night. Do you have some towels that we can use to make a bed for Ragnar? I forgot his pad. I’ll make popcorn, I managed to remember that, and I brought a bottle of wine. Let’s get this all figured out.” She soothes me.

I move to make preparations for Ragnar, while she handles the other items. Changing into her pajamas, as I’m already in sweats for the night, we sit across from each other on the bed and I unload. I know she’s at least twenty years older than me, but she’s amazing. She listens, she keeps me on track, and then she weighs in. As I start to calm down, I realize I basically know nothing about her.

“Bree, can I ask, where are you from? Do you have children? I feel so bad to just throw all of this at you.” I take a deep breath and a calming sip of wine.

“I’ve lived lots of places. I wasn’t lucky enough to have a child, but I’m really, really good at being an Aunt. I was married a bit later in life and before I knew it he was taken from me. I wound up here last summer and met Flint, who’s a force of nature in his own right.” She smiles at me and I can see the love that she has for him reflected on her face.

“Flint was pretty, um, intense, the other night.”

“He was kind of an ass to you. Let’s just put that out there.” It must be the wine, but I start giggling. “I hadn’t arrived here prior to you and Gunner originally meeting, but let me say, I’ve never seen him with another woman. Not that I’m around the clubhouse, or him, twenty-four-seven, but the guys would heckle him about his monk status. Hell, if he cheats on you, I’ll help you plot his demise.”

We both start laughing. As it’s getting late, we lie down. Bree promises to drive me back and forth to school the next day. I’m too tired to argue.

GUNNER

All in all, the run went smoothly. I hate dealing with the crew from California, but the weather seems to have kept all the wolves and pigs at bay. I was watching my phone, worried about any news from Riley and the guys, but all seems quiet.

Pulling into the clubhouse, I'm anxious to get the briefing with Jas over with and get home. Sitting in a corner with Jake, Connal signals me immediately, but Vice motions for me to join him in the office. As the low man on the run, Royce hits the bar. Vice and I let Jas know the score and get a timeline for the next deal. Connal and Hawk are next up, and we debate sending the probie with them.

Jas finally looks at me and tells me that Connal is waiting to talk to me, gladly taking my dismissal I head out to the bar to talk to him.

"You're going to want this." It's not the best start when he has to give me whiskey before the news. I accept it and raise an eyebrow so he'll get started. "Turns out her parents arrived the day you left. They reclaimed her SUV the next day." He fills me in on Riley's week and I signal for another drink. "...so she called Bree."

"Good."

"Yeah, Bree went straight there and spent the night. Riley called me in the morning, and I set her up with the loaner car I keep at the garage. She gave me a budget, not a lot, but asked me to help her find something dependable to drive. I have something but been dragging my heels on that till I got your input. She said she could do seven thousand tops."

"Double that. Make sure it's safe and dependable. And

don't fucking tell her I'm contributing, I'll tell her if she asks."

"In that case, I have something I can show you tomorrow. Older guy, doesn't drive much and had already asked me to help sell his truck cause with arthritis getting in and out is hard on him. He's asking twelve. Then let's see, Friday night she was at her Grams. I hung around and followed her home. She started crying when she got in the car, but I just tailed her home and took off after she was inside.

"I gave her a call this morning to let her know I was checking on a vehicle for her and see if she needed anything. She sounded good, said Flint had just called her and she was stuck at home waiting for a sofa to be delivered. Said she'd have me over for dinner when she had a place for me to sit. Do you know if she can cook?" He looks hopeful. We're usually all trying to find a place for a home-cooked meal.

"We mostly eat out, she did pasta one night, I don't know. Thanks, Connal. I owe you."

"You really don't, you know that. But if she can cook, then I do want an invite!" Laughing, I hit him on the shoulder. Turning to leave I see Frank. Fuck me. I haven't seen him since last week and need to square that shit.

Walking over to the booth, I see he's getting blown by Deb but he motions me over anyway.

"That was bullshit," Frank grunts at me, reaching a hand around Deb's head to control her rhythm.

"You're right, I shouldn't have hit you. I wasn't expecting to see her here and overreacted. It won't happen again but let me be absolutely clear: no one touches her but me." I growl at him, not caring who's listening.

"Fuck, Gunner, that's downright unfriendly, not sharing an ass like that." He laughs, half panting over the job Deb is doing on him. Before I can knock the shit out of him again, Connal is almost on top of us.

"We all friends here, Brothers?" He drawls out. "Gunner, come to the garage tomorrow at eleven for that test drive, it's all set." He stands there as Frank looks between the two of us, then decides to pull Deb up from under the table, settling her on his dick. He smirks up at me, like I fucking give a shit about her ass.

I head out behind Connal.

"You can't hit him again until you claim her, you moron," he smirks at me.

"But it'd really feel good." We laugh then part ways. I shoot Riley a quick text before heading to her place.

As I pull up, there is a large truck, a squad car, and the regular Saturday shoppers outside her place. With no parking in sight, I pull around to the spots in back and let myself in the back door with the extra key she gave me.

CHAPTER EIGHTEEN

GUNNER

"This isn't a good time, Officer," is the first thing I hear. Riley sounds more annoyed than anything, so I continue into the front room.

"All good, Sweetheart?" I decide to announce my entrance before I get to the end of the hallway. The front room has two guys unwrapping a sofa, a third coming through the door with an oversized ottoman, and Officer Kennelly standing near the kitchen island. Everyone has frozen and turned to stare my way.

Riley's face lights up and she quickly closes the distance between us.

"Gunner! I wanted to surprise you but..." she indicates the furniture, then the nuisance in the kitchen area.

"What are you doing here, Sorenson?" Kennelly cuts in.

"I believe I'm welcome here, what about you?" I stand, holding Riley to my body and staring the officer down. I have no real problem with cops in general but this one is an all-around pain in the ass.

"He came up when I let the delivery guys in," Riley explains.

"I'm here on an authorized wellness check. Riley's family is concerned about her and considering the company..." Mr. High and Mighty starts spouting before my girl cuts in.

"Enough! I am an adult, Officer. I was at my Grandmother's last night and she expressed no concern for my well-being. I have already asked you to leave and I will be calling the sheriff. You have no right tracking me down because I'm upset with my parents and won't return their call." While I had every intention of handling this, I do love seeing her fight her own battles.

As Kennelly flushes, remembering the presence of the three delivery guys who have paused to watch the show, he starts stammering about this being a legitimate complaint. Riley simply points to the door, so he replaces his hat and heads out mumbling to himself.

"Gentlemen, I believe there's one more piece?" She turns this last bit on the delivery guys to get them moving again and I don't waste a moment picking Riley up and putting her on the island. Kissing her thoroughly, letting her feel how much I missed her. Lost in her arms, I step back when we're asked where to place an extra wide upholstered chair. Riley points, jumping down to inspect it. Tipping the workers then signing off on some paperwork, she locks the door behind them. "Do you like them, Gunner?"

"I need you. Couch or bed, Sweetheart?" I ask, pulling off my clothes.

RILEY

"Sit here," I indicate the large chair. Watching Gunner cross the space and sit down, I reach up under my long skirt and remove my panties. Keeping my skirt up, I move to sit on him but pause as I see he's fumbling with a condom.

I quickly seek to impale myself on him. Moaning, I feel as tight as I was the other night.

"Easy there, Sweetheart," he lifts my shirt over my head and lightly nibbles on each breast. "I know how to get you wet, then you just slide on down."

With a knee on either side of him, I gently bounce on his cock. Overly eager to feel all of him inside me again, my pussy is soon wet enough to help him get fully seated. I sit still for a moment, grinding my clit against his pelvic bone.

"Ride me, Sweetheart. Really. Fucking. Hard!" Gunner strangles out and I'm off.

My inexperience causes me to lift off his cock a few times but I eventually set as fast a pace as I can manage and between his cock hitting all the way up to my cervix and him sucking my nipples through my lacy bra, I'm coming before I know it. Slumped over him, he leans over to kiss me, slipping his tongue in to take possession of my mouth as his dick still throbs inside me.

Then with one hand behind me, he leans my nearly limp body back so I'm mostly lying on the ottoman. Moving to the edge of the chair, he says, "My turn." Then pounds into me until his release comes, his eyes don't leave mine and the fierce need I see in them brings me a second crashing orgasm as he finishes while yelling my name.

Standing with me in his arms, his gradually softening cock still inside me, he walks over the kitchen before setting me back on the island. Dumping the condom, and grabbing a dishtowel to wipe me off, he picks me up, this time cradling me in his arms before moving back to the new chair.

"I fucking love this chair." He smiles down at me while holding me close and protected against his naked body.

I can't help but laugh and all the stress from the past few days completely dissipates.

"Riley, I'm sorry I wasn't here for you." I put my finger over his mouth but he merely kisses it before pulling it away. "Connal told me what he knew and I feel like shit I couldn't be here to ease your load."

"Gunner, this was all going to happen regardless of you. The only difference is, because of you, I'm staying here now and will have to deal with them." Taking a breath, "I didn't even consider they'd take the SUV back and strand me in the middle of winter!

"Gram said to give it a day or so before reaching out to them, but agrees with me that they're more upset about how this will look to their associates than anything else. Mom actually told her she must have dementia and should be evaluated! Rogers is beside himself thinking they may try to get her out of the way."

"There's no way anyone can spend five minutes with her and think there's anything off! She's as sharp as they come, I mean other than thinking I'm perfect for you." I narrow my eyes at him as he grins down at me.

"Not funny right now, Baby," I say as he nuzzles me and nips my ear.

"Baby? You've never called me anything but Gunner?" He raises an eyebrow at me.

"Would you prefer Alex?" I laugh as he flinches.

"Put that way, I can live with Baby, just so long as you as only scream 'Gunner' when you come."

"Deal." I start kissing his neck, mewling when he pushes me back.

"Let's talk this out before round two, Sweetheart." He

kisses my forehead as I sigh. "I spoke to Connal and there's a solid truck he wants you to test drive tomorrow morning, so that's step one."

"Next, I've been thinking about the space downstairs. I want to talk to a couple people I know and maybe we pitch in together to rent the store? Anne has her jewelry line, my furniture, and I know a cousin of one of the other Ol' Lady's has a pottery/glassblowing line. If the three of us sell out of one space and split the rent, I think we will clear more than what we have to pay out in commissions to retailers carrying our designs. Flint has a strong head for business so I just want to get his perspective on how this would work. Do you have a sample lease that I can show him?" He asks, obviously having given this some thought.

"I think that's a great idea! Like an artists' cooperative? Gram told me what the rent should be for me to clear expenses, build a sort of maintenance fund for the building and have some income, but I can discount that..." I start, getting excited about his plan.

"No. Absolutely not. If the number doesn't sound fair we'll talk, but your Gram knows the going rates around here and we'll stick to it," Gunner insists.

"Then I'll use it to pay you for a dining set. Don't roll your eyes at me! I'm serious. You work hard and if I can't give you a discount, then I don't get one." I'm pointing my finger at him by the end of that outburst and he leans down to take it in his mouth.

As I struggle to turn to straddle him, he holds me still again. "Not yet, Ri. Third topic: your parents. I don't want Kennelly parked outside day and night. You've got to call them. They already know about me, so maybe we meet them for an early dinner somewhere tomorrow?"

"So handsome, so naïve," I say, in my most condescending voice, patting him on his head like a child.

"Ha! Since I'm not handsome, I'm obviously not naïve either," he says chuckling.

"I think you're very good looking, Gunner. So don't say that about yourself," I gasp, actually upset about this trivial point.

"Sweetheart, I'm happy I do it for you but I wasn't good looking even before I stopped a bomb with my face. Now, do you want to call them before or after I stick my dick inside you again?"

"After!" I eagerly respond.

"Promise?" He says as he stands up, setting me to the side he heads back to the bedroom. "Stay there, I'm not done with that chair yet!" He calls over his shoulder. "Just need more condoms."

Well, I'm glad he likes my purchases. I smile to myself as I remove my skirt and bra.

GUNNER

After teaching my Sweetheart about riding a reverse cowgirl on me, we slowly move to the shower. Before long, I'm on my knees before her getting her off with my tongue and fingers, my thumb sliding in and out of her tight asshole I've yet to claim.

Looking up at Riley, head thrown back under the rain shower head, I'm again amazed at her capacity to give herself over to me so completely. Thankful for her, I pull her close, kissing her belly button and secretly hoping I got her pregnant the other night; knowing how unfair that would be to her at this time in her life and feeling ashamed of myself.

"Are you hungry?" She asks, stirring me from my

thoughts when I'm finally wrapping her in a towel. I guess I really only notice when towels are too small for me, but the ones she bought are huge and easily circle my waist so it nearly swallows her. "I marinated some chicken breasts. I can stick those in the oven."

"Grill." I get out, as I start to brush my teeth. "I got to get a grill for that deck. But sure, oven will work tonight."

Slipping one of my t-shirts over her head she heads back out to the great room. There's something else we have to discuss.

"Riley, I came here today without really asking." She looks up at me with her eyebrows knitted together. "How do you want this to work? I want to be with you, but this is your place and I don't want to crowd you, so what should I plan on? A few nights a week here? Do you just want to take it day by day?"

Getting dinner in the oven, she's avoiding eye contact and I'm not sure why.

"I should probably call my parents now. You sure you want to meet with us tomorrow? I can do it alone," she says quietly.

Reaching out for her phone, I take it and hold it above her head as she tries walking past me. "Riley, what's going on in that head of yours?" She shrugs.

"Don't fucking shrug at me, tell me what you want."

"Don't yell at me!" Ok, now I do see her eyes misting over.

"Hey! Hey, don't get mad. I'm just trying to figure out what you expect from me, when I should give you space? You know?" I try to wrap an arm around her.

"Flint said you would want space, I just didn't think it would happen in the first week." She storms down to her bedroom and I have no idea what just happened. Taking a deep breath, I lower the temperature on the oven and as I brace myself to head after her, her phone rings. It's her father.

What the fuck, might as well do this now.

"Riley's phone." My answer is met with silence.

"Who is this?"

"Gunner, Riley's in the other room."

"Alexander "Gunner" Sorenson, I'm having you investigated for statutory rape." Funny how this man's voice makes me what to pull him through the phone and beat the shit out of him.

"Yeah, good luck with that. We got together for the first time last Saturday. Say, how'd you spend your daughter's birthday?"

"Go to hell."

"Look, we're getting off on the wrong foot here." I look up to see Riley watching me from the hallway. "Riley was actually about to call you and your wife. We'd like to have an early dinner with you both tomorrow, here in town, sort of clear the air a bit."

"We don't want you anywhere near her, Riley can come out here to discuss..."

Holding the phone away from my ear, I loudly ask Riley; "Sweetheart, they don't seem to want me around you, do you want to talk to your father?" He and I wait for her reply.

I surrender the phone, as she comes towards it. "Hi, Father," she says in a softer voice than I'm used to hearing from her, one devoid of any emotion. Keeping her eyes on me as she listens, I can hear indistinguishable words and his voice getting louder and louder. Finally, there is silence until she replies using that same hollow tone of voice.

"I've been very disappointed by you and mother over the

years, so I can, indeed, understand how you feel right now. Perhaps you'll get over it, like I did?

"If so, text me a restaurant and time you would like to meet Gunner and I and we will sit down with you and mother. In the future, I would ask that you keep a civil tone and language when speaking to me. Good night." She disconnects the call. I stand staring at her in amazement. I would never have been able to keep my cool, through what I expect, was quite a tirade.

"Please tell me why you're upset with me?" I open my arms to her, not making a move otherwise.

Throwing herself into my arms, she says, "I'm sorry. I, this, you, it's my first relationship and I just want to be close to you. I just want you here. Flint said something that upset me the other night and I just, well, do you want to be here? To stay here with me?"

"It's pretty much my first relationship also. I just didn't want to basically move in with you without asking. I want to be with you too. What did Flint say?"

"Just asked what I would do the next time you get drunk and end up fucking someone else. That it would happen, "it's just the life." Bree told me he was an ass and to forget it. But I stood up for you to him and he looked at me like I was so naïve." Taking a deep breath, she continues. "I don't want to be cling wrap, so if you want to stay at the club I get that you might need space, just remember your promise. And also, Bree said she'd help me hide your body if you cheated on me."

Chuckling, though I'm sure Bree would junk punch me at the very least. "I've had space. Years and years of space. Can I just be here with you and you'll tell me if I'm annoying the crap out of you?" She smiles up at me, nodding.

"Only if you tell me when I annoy you?" Riley says, cupping my cheek.

"That's not how this works, Sweetheart! If you annoy me, I'll take you over my knee." I wiggle my eyebrows at her, knowing we're back on track.

Thirty minutes later, I've polished off three chicken breasts plus her sautéed garlic spinach and I'm looking for my phone.

"What are you doing?" Riley tilts her head at me in question.

"I have to text Connal," I say, with my last bite still in my mouth.

She frowns at me, "Anything wrong?"

"No. He wanted to take you up on that home cooked meal you offered if I vouched for your cooking. This was fucking good!" She's laughing at me while I text Connal. Getting up I set the first house rule—the cook doesn't clean the dishes.

CHAPTER NINETEEN

RILEY

THE NEXT MORNING I SLIDE OUT OF BED AS GUNNER LIES snoring. Grabbing a Diet Coke and heading to the couch, I call the town police department and ask for the sheriff. Turns out, Sunday mornings are very slow and the sheriff answered the phone himself.

"Oh, I thought I'd be on hold forever!" I say after announcing myself.

"Huh. Do Maddocks get put on hold anywhere? Especially not a Riley-Maddock in this town, I'm guessing?" Was hardly the reply I was expecting.

"Um, well, I have a concern and wanted to discuss it with you, without any fallout," I start, and he grunts. "So I just turned eighteen," another grunt on the other end of the line. "My Gram, well she gave me one of her properties and it had an apartment above it, so I immediately moved into it."

"Jesus Christ, Girl. I'm the sheriff, not a relocation specialist," he growls.

"Wait! Please. My parents, well, they've been working with Officer Kennelly and he came here yesterday when I had buzzed delivery men in and said something about a wellness check that was on record for me. I had dinner with my gram on Friday night, so that was ridiculous. I don't think he would have left so easily if the man I'm seeing hadn't arrived."

"Who are you dating?"

"Gunner Sorenson. My gram's known him forever," I throw in, trying to diffuse the MC connection. "Then my father calls last night and tells him that he's having him investigated for statutory rape, which is untrue. I approached Gunner on my birthday last Saturday."

"And now you're dating him?" I swear I hear him drawing circles on a paper out of boredom.

"Please. I need you to take this seriously. Does Kennelly have any right to come into a building I own, without permission, and ask me questions?" After a brief sigh, he asks me to hold on and then I hear him typing for a few moments.

"No, there aren't any notes in the system about you. I will speak to Kennelly about this and put a notice in his file. You are correct, he had no right to force his way in. Can anyone else, other than Gunner, verify this?"

"Yes! The three delivery guys were within ten feet of us and definitely listening."

"I have to ask you about the statutory rape issue, Miss Maddock. What will your parents find?"

"Nothing, Sir. There is nothing to find. Again, my gram will vouch for Gunner, but my parents are upset with me and I don't think they'll back down easily."

"You sound reasonably intelligent, and while Gunner has never been tried or convicted of any crime, you must know something about the MC? About what kind of man he is?" He asks, although he still sounds slightly bored.

"You mean other than him being a decorated Vet?" I ask and get another sigh in response. "He's a good man, Sheriff, and now he's mine," I look over my shoulder to see Gunner watching me.

Walking towards me, he holds out his hand for the phone. "Sheriff Michaels? Everything alright?" He listens to the sheriff for a few moments. "Not just going to be my Ol' Lady, Sheriff," Gunner says, looking at me without blinking. "I'm going to marry her. I already cleared it with Mrs. Riley."

My jaw is gaping open. Then I scream at him, smacking his shoulder.

Seriously, he announces it to the sheriff before asking me?! He grunts out, "Shit, gotta let you go." He disconnects the call as I try to swat him again.

He swings me up into his arms and tries apologizing. "I told you, you are mine! Of course, I'm marrying you, Sweetheart."

That doesn't really cut it right now.

"No, you have to ask. I have to say yes. You don't get to tell anyone shit like that before we decide it together, you freaking Caveman!"

"I think I like 'Baby' better." He smirks at me.

"Whatever, ALEX," I say, launching myself off his lap.

I head to the bedroom to get dressed. This calls for a Ray's Diner #6, and I will eat it all. He pads back to the bedroom, checking to see if it's safe and I give him three minutes to get dressed and join me for breakfast.

"I love you," Gunner calls as I head up toward the door. The tone of his voice makes it sound an awful lot like I'm sorry.

GUNNER

What the hell did she think I was playing at here? I wonder as she shoots me another glare over a fork full of pancakes. I smile at her, I learned my lesson last time—no way I will ever order the #6 again.

"And my gram?" She mutters to herself, taking a hard bite into a sausage link. I've decided silence is the best answer right now. She's so damn cute all worked up like this, I can't help the smile on my face. Noticing Margie staring at me, I tone it down and dig back into my own breakfast.

Looking around the diner, I notice a couple guys from the MC looking the worse for wear after the night before. They give me a nod, which I acknowledge with a glare, catching Riley's attention in the meanwhile.

"Please, don't tell me Kennelly is back there?" She asks as her shoulders tense up.

"No, Sweetheart, just some of my Brothers. They're all straining to get a look at your face now, so it's kinda funny." I smirk at her.

"Should I stand up and let them check me out?" She smirks right back at me.

"Hell no, they want to act like nosy old women, don't make it easy on them!" I stare across the room until they take the hint to mind themselves. "So, this truck today, Connal's done all the work on it and its really low mileage. I think it'll be just what you need. Um, I forgot to ask but did you bring the money? Or how do you want to arrange that?"

"What? Oh, no. I already gave the money to Connal." My jaw has dropped and I don't know what to say. Seeing how frustrated I am, she quickly continues. "Gunner, what if he found something and couldn't get a hold of me right away?"

"You just handed him seven thousand dollars? Sweetheart, you have to be more careful." I pinch together the bridge of my nose. I know she doesn't view money like the majority of us and we will have to have this discussion, gently, another time.

"Gunner, you said I could trust him! I wouldn't give it to just anyone." She sounds exasperated and I'm slightly dumbfounded by this statement.

"So if I tell you someone is trustworthy, you'd just let them hold onto thousands of dollars for you?" I choke out.

"Not at all. But the way you talk about Connal is different, than, well, say, Wrench, for instance. I haven't met Wrench yet, and you haven't said anything bad about him but you don't talk about him the same way you do Connal. Besides, Connal flipped out when I gave him the money before he had anything lined up for me, so that confirmed it that he wasn't going to swindle me," she explains and her reasoning stuns me.

"You aren't wrong. I trust Connal completely. Jesus, even the thought of you driving around with that kind of money freaks me out. People have killed for less, Sweetheart. I just need you to be cautious, alright?" Suddenly, she seems really interested in her empty plate and I just know I don't want to hear what she's thinking. Especially not with people around us, I wave Marge over for the check and settle up.

Reaching over to help her stand, and still seeing a sheepish look on her face, I pull her straight up to my mouth and take complete possession of hers. My Brothers, down on the other side, start hooting and soon most of the customers start laughing along with them. Over the ruckus, Margie yells at me to keep it PG. Pulling back, Riley's cheeks are all pink and I realize I've done nothing but frustrate myself. There's no time to stop home to take care of the intense pressure in my pants.

Getting into the truck, I turn to look at her as I start it up. "Do you happen to have a stockpile of cash at the apartment?"

"How did you know?"

"From the look on your face back there. Fuck," I groan.

"I had always put my allowance in the bank but have been slowly taking it out the past few months. As a minor, my father's name was on my account. I took the balance of it out last week. I bought a lockbox for it when you were out of town."

"Tomorrow morning, we'll drive to the bank near your school and deposit the bulk of it there, ok?" She readily agrees and leans over to kiss my cheek, as we pull into the lot for Connal's Garage.

CHAPTER TWENTY

GUNNER

STANDING NEXT TO CONNAL AND A PRISTINE CHEVY Colorado, is an older man who looks vaguely familiar. I know I'm being studied as I walk around the truck to get Riley from the passenger side. As we approach them, the man steps forward.

"I can guess whose boy you are. You look a lot like him." He sticks his hand out to shake mine. "Hopefully, you're a better man than he is and take real good care of this one." While he isn't much taller than Riley, he holds my hand and my stare with his own.

With no patience for testosterone poisoning, Riley extends her own hand. "Hi, I'm Riley Maddock."

Turning to acknowledge her, he raises an eyebrow at her. "Well, you both got shit for parents then, didn't ya?"

Riley throws her head back laughing, instantly putting Connal and me at ease again. "We really did!" She readily agrees. "But our grandmothers made up for that."

Still taking her measure, he replies, "You're too young to

have known him, but your grandfather was a good man also. I'm Andy Weston. Worked for him some twenty odd years. Hard man, but fair."

Connal's likely to make himself dizzy, trying to keep up between Andy's exchange with us and our reactions. Speaking up he starts going over what he knows about the vehicle, with Andy nodding along. I'd already texted Connal not to mention the asking price.

"Great, can I take it out for a test run?" Riley asks when Connal winds down. Andy hands her the keys, and I walk her over to the driver side.

"Do you mind if I hang back?" I check with her.

"Sure, everything's alright?"

"Yeah, just want to shoot the shit with this guy for a bit. Gimme some sugar." She melts into me for a kiss. I really can't wait to get her home.

The three of us head into the garage to keep warm while Riley tests out the truck.

"You're looking for twelve grand?" I confirm with Andy.

"Seems weird she doesn't have a vehicle already," Andy is trying to get a grasp on us.

"Her parents took back the truck they'd given her. Her budget is less than you're asking, but I'll take care of the balance. I want her to have something dependable."

"Her grandfather was good to me, eleven will do. Cash though," he says and I pause, not knowing what to say to this offer. That number is well below book. "He'd have wanted her to have something dependable also." He continues, staring me down. I nod, the double meaning in his statement is not lost on me.

Connal comes from the office with the envelope of cash she had given him. I count out my own money and add it to Riley's envelope. "All set, as long as she's happy with it."

An hour later, we're pulling up in front of the apartment. Connal jumps out of my truck to drive his loaner car back to the garage.

"Connal, do you like lasagna? I can make that for you tonight if you want to come back around six or so?" Riley offers.

"Sounds great!" Connal readily accepts.

"No," I interject at the same time. "We have plans tonight. Come tomorrow night."

"Gunner, what plans?" Riley is unlocking the door and doesn't see the hungry look on my face. Connal laughs and confirms the next night. Picking her up, I kick the door closed behind us and head up the stairs.

"Gunner! That was rude. He really helped me out!" She shrieks, grabbing the waistband of my jeans.

"What about me?! I haven't been inside you all day," I ask, in as pained tone of voice as I can manage. Unlocking the upstairs door, I head straight to the kitchen island and deposit her there. Pushing her back, I wrestle with the buttons on her jeans and pull them down over her hips.

"Take your top off, Sweetheart, I want to see you playing with those peach colored nipples every time I look up."

I bury my face in her sweet, hot cunt. Holding her folds apart with my fingers, I thrust my tongue right up into her wet center. Within a moment, she is soaking my face with her honey and I slide her wetness up to stroke her nub with my finger.

I cannot get enough of her, I continue to devour her past her orgasm. Moving up to suck her clit into my mouth, I stroke that with my tongue. Dipping my finger into her center, I spread her moisture down to her asshole and use the lubricant to start inserting my finger in a steady rhythm, ever deeper and deeper. Like each time before, she lurches up when I first breach her tight ring, but before long she eases the stranglehold on my finger and starts to scream in earnest as she comes a second time.

Unzipping my jeans, I ease my finger out of her ass to get a wrapper on my cock. Drawing my thumb through her wet folds, I move it down and start working that digit into her tight back hole as I slide one of her legs up onto my shoulder. Aiming my cock into her pussy, I thrust all the way up in one motion.

She gasps but returns my gaze with half-hooded eyes. "Who owns this pussy, Riley?" I growl at her, desperate to hear the words.

She moans and I'm not even sure she understands me after coming twice so close together. "I won't fucking move until you tell me whose pretty pussy this is, Sweetheart!" I repeat harshly, reaching up to tweak a rock hard nipple.

"Yours, Gunner!" Riley cries out, trying to grind herself on my solid length as it pulses against her tight walls.

"My what?"

"It's your pussy, Gunner, I belong to you. My ass, Gunner, that too. Please. I need you. Please," as she whimpers on. Becoming more and more incoherent I slowly thrust in and out of her knowing it won't take me long to burst. I know memories of seeing her like this, making her like this, will stay with me all my life and all I want is for her to come a third time, this time squeezing my dick dry.

RILEY

A short while later, Gunner has me settled between his legs in the oversized tub, with the air jets swirling the hot water around us.

My body still humming from my orgasms. I bring his

hand to my lips. "I meant it, Gunner." Referring to what I said earlier.

"I'll ask you properly, you know?" He nuzzles against my neck. "When it's time, I'll get down on my knee and everything, Sweetheart."

Turning my head to lay kisses over his chest, I can't stop grinning to myself. "I shouldn't have gotten mad at you this morning. Just the way you said it, was like it was already settled."

"I can see it so clearly, Riley. I didn't mean to take you for granted, I guess it didn't occur to me you didn't know my thoughts. How could I not want to marry a woman who can eat Ray's #6 twice a week? OUCH!" He barks out after I had swung my elbow back.

"Serves you right!" I say, grinning up at him as he inspects my elbow.

"Damn, that thing is sharp!" He laughs. Taking my hand and wrapping it around his cock, he nibbles on my earlobe. "Want to review some of what you've learned so far?"

CHAPTER TWENTY-ONE

RILEY

THE NEXT MORNING STARTS WITH A LITTLE ARGUMENT ABOUT money since I only want to deposit part of my cash. We finally settle on splitting it into thirds between a safety deposit box, a checking account, and leaving the rest in the lockbox. The last part I really had to push for and it was settled with the caveat that Gunner would open up some of the drywall and hide it in the wall.

Then he followed me to the bank like a hired gun, which is technically part of his job description with the MC. Our next argument ensued when I put his name down as someone who could access the safety deposit box. He was adamant he wanted no part of my money. I won that round, but after he signed the paperwork, he whispered in my ear that would come with a punishment. I finished the meeting beet red; the banker very politely pretended not to notice.

We part, me to school and Gunner leaving to get some work done at the shop and check in at the clubhouse. My later class is cancelled due to a faulty heater, so I take the time to catch up on my studies in the library. As much as I'm becoming addicted to the strings of orgasms Gunner doles out, I can't allow myself to fall behind.

A light tap on my shoulder interrupts me and the girl who had invited me to the ill-fated party nearly a year ago asks to join me. I was quiet with her at first, I know I became persona non grata around campus after the party but I had really missed having someone to discuss coursework with and we easily fell into a whispered reunion.

Telling Kristy that I had finally turned eighteen had her miming wiping her brow and grinning broadly at me. "So, I work as a teller at the bank part time," she said giving me serious side eye. "Who was that guy you came in with today?"

"I guess he's my boyfriend," I say, not really knowing how to classify him.

"Seriously? I thought he was coming in to rob us when I first saw him! Wow." She notices me tensing at her comment. That or the narrowing of my eyes. "I'm sorry! I'm sorry. He's just like seriously HUGE. Gosh, you went from seventeen to eighteen really fast, didn't you?! Not that you ever seemed that much younger than us."

"Yeah, we met on my birthday and it's pretty intense. My Gram has known him forever, and if she doesn't object and I'm really happy..." I shrug, not interested in saying anything else.

She exhales and looks around. Suddenly she digs through her bag for a notepad and starts writing out several paragraphs, while aimlessly chatting about a professor we had.

Tearing the page off, she slides it to me; continuing to chatter on. Looking down, I feel instantly nauseous.

There's a guy walking around campus showing your picture. Once I said I knew u, he offered me cash to bring back a recording of u talking about a guy named Gunner. He wants information on anything before last week.

Let me know if I can help – and she signed her name and number.

When I look back up at her, she indicated her mobile phone, face down on the table and I know we're being recorded.

"Well, it was great catching up with you!" I say for the benefit of the recording while holding her arm. She's clever enough to say goodbye, turn off the mic and slip it into her bag.

"Let's go to the bathroom?" I say, not knowing who else is around. We gather our things and head in together, making sure we're alone.

"Thank you so much for telling me! My parents have just gone off the deep end." I say as I splash water on my face.

"So, what you said, your grandmother? She does know him and you are ok, right?" Kristy confirms.

"Truly." I turn to look her in the eye so there won't be any doubt. "Look, I have to go run some errands, but maybe we could have lunch tomorrow? Cafeteria about noon? I'll text you my number, alright?"

We make our plans and I head out. I know Gunner is busy plus there's nothing he can do about this now anyway, so I just go to the grocery store and get started on dinner. Gram calls as I'm putting the lasagna in the oven.

"Just checking in on you, Dear?" Some days, today included, Gram's voice is like my very own security blanket.

I try to keep control of my voice as I catch her up on the last couple days.

“That was why I was calling, Riley. Sheriff Michaels made an appointment to see me this afternoon. Naturally, the last thing he wants is a pissing match between the Governor’s office and the Motorcycle Club. I told him I would handle it before it got that far.” I can almost hear a smile in her voice and wonder what she’s up to. “Now, so you’re aware, Officer Kennelly did not take the criticism of his treatment of you very well, insisting he was within his rights. He has been put on unpaid leave for three days.”

I groan, knowing this is going to get worse before it gets better. “So, he has three full days where no other work will stop him from following me around?”

“I’m afraid so, but this also points to who was at the university today and you can talk to campus security about that. If it is him, I will have my attorney look into a restraining order against him. The threat of that and the repercussions with his job should jolt some sense into the overeager officer,” she assures me.

“Gram. I didn’t mean for World War Three to break out over my relationship. I knew it wouldn’t be easy, but they don’t care about me. Why not just let it be?”

“With someone from a different walk of life, they would have. It could even have been spun with their associates to make them look sympathetic, just not with someone with Gunner’s ties.” She sighs, and shifts the phone, saying something to Rogers. “You are happy, aren’t you, Riley? That’s what I want for you. And as unpolished as Gunner is, I also know he is a good person, a loyal man. I want this next part of your life to be everything you deserve.”

I start crying then, telling gram that I am happy and thanking her for her faith before she ends the call.

Realizing the time, I take a quick shower and change before the guys get here for dinner. When the doorbell rings, I immediately buzz them in, a little surprised that Connal beat Gunner here. Peeking out the door, Connal is maneuvering chairs into the door and looks up at me. "Hey! Gunner has the table in his truck but had me pick these up. Just give me a minute."

Moving back, I hold the door and shake my head at Gunner's thoughtfulness. I had set places on the coffee table, thinking we could make do there.

"Holy shit it smells great up here!" Connal exclaims after his second trip carrying chairs up. "Gunner has more chairs for the table back at the shop, but these should get us through tonight." He crosses to the sink to wash his hands. Then he watches me as I uncover the lasagna and put it back in the oven to finish baking.

"I wanted to talk to you about something." He looks really uncomfortable now. "You know he and I are tight, right?" I nod, getting nervous. "Look, you seem like a good person, but with your family and all, I gotta say, if Gunner claims you, you can't just break up with him at the first sign of trouble.

"That's just not how we are. We have to know we can trust you and none of us know you. Gunner's not thinking with his big head right now. I want you to really think hard about what life would be like if Gunner ever gets shot or arrested or anything else. Can you stick through that?" He looks at me, genuinely curious.

"I've had a rough day, Connal, and before that, I had eight months to read up on biographies from motorcycle gang members, women who were traded around, internet searches on everything I could find on those of you with records. I know life with Gunner is going to be more than multiple orgasms every day. And as everyone likes to point out, my parents aren't going to make this easy either," I reply as I aggressively grate more parmesan cheese.

Ok, maybe I shouldn't have mentioned multiple orgasms, but it's not like my man has ever given me flowers. Connal looks distracted now. "Right now, I have one 'do not cross' line with Gunner, and he's agreed to it. If he breaks it I'm gone. Otherwise, I'm all in."

We stand staring at each other. "Just if you have any doubt, Riley, you have to cut it off immediately. Before he claims you." I nod in reply to his advice. Smirking at me, he continues "It's not the toilet seat, is it? My Ma used to get so pissed about the damn toilet seat!"

I laugh, throwing my oven mitt at him, appreciating his attempt to move on from the topic. "It's not. I figure if he's able to lift it up, I should be clever enough to put it down. BUT...never sharing a bathroom with a man before, I will say it is not fun landing in the toilet when you stumble out of bed in the middle of the night to pee."

Connal laughs at the visual, then we turn as we hear the key in the door. Gunner comes in carrying the table legs, "Hey Sweetheart! Connal, come help me with the other pieces?"

I cross over to kiss him, feeling the stress of the day and knowing he will make me feel better. Laying the legs down, he wraps me in his arms and thoroughly kisses me. "I missed you," I say softly.

"You alright, Riley?" I nod and nudge him downstairs after Connal. Crossing to the fridge, I remove two trays of my unbaked chocolate chip cookie dough that I'll put in the oven once I take the lasagna out.

They go back down after they get the table top up, returning with tools, whiskey, beer, and wine.

GUNNER

Reassembling the table in the great goom and looking around really makes me feel good. I know we have a ways to go, but Riley and I have a comfortably furnished space.

"Gunner! That table is beautiful! And it's the same wood as the coffee table, isn't it?" Riley slips her arm around my waist as she admires the woodwork.

"Yeah, yeah, your guy is fantastic. Blah blah blah," Connal contributes, holding up the bottle of Jack. "Where can I find a glass? Gunner, whiskey or beer? Riley, apple juice for you, right?"

"Jack for me. Riley, I got you red or white wine, which do you prefer?"

"Y'know, I'll have what you're having," she says resolutely, moving for the glasses. I grab hers and add a healthy dose of ice with a splash of water. I want to be holding her hair when I enter her later, not when she's hanging over a toilet, so I glare at Connal as he makes a comment about the 'police state' Riley lives in.

She has me dish up the lasagna. She's thought of everything with freshly grated parmesan and red pepper flakes on the table. Connal and I groan loudly after the first bite. Giving her a big nod, we seriously dig in. Riley quietly switches to wine after her first whiskey and sits back to watch us eat, telling us about a cyber-attack that was discussed in her morning lecture.

"Jesus Christ, Riley! Where'd you learn to cook?" Connal asks, finally taking a breath after his second helping.

"I learned Italian food from my housekeeper/nanny, Rosa, from the time I was ten to twelve. Mexican foods and breads, I learned from Esme who they hired for the next two years. Then Donna came after her and she showed me a little of everything and desserts. I've never cooked for anyone other than myself. You really like it?"

"Shit, you're like the best-kept secret in town!" Connal says while contemplating a third helping. "Gunner, remember that little Italian place we went to in Chicago? This is even better!"

Smiling at Riley as she looks up at me, "Thank you for making this for us, Sweetheart. It really is the best I've ever had." The light in her eyes warms me up more than the whiskey. Company here or not, I can't help but draw her in for a long kiss.

"Save room for dessert, Connal!" She warns as I let her up for air. "I'll send leftovers home with you."

"What?! No! I want the leftovers," I yell, getting a slug in the shoulder from Connal.

"I can make it for you anytime though," she reasons.

"Oh, I'm happy to come over anytime." Frowning at Connal's statement, I've decided he's no longer welcome here. He and Riley just laugh when I growl, then he continues. "Maybe Jake can come next time?"

"I didn't know you were seeing someone, Connal?" Riley asks, suddenly frowning as I throw my head back laughing and Connal turns purple choking on his drink.

"Jake's in the MC. He and Connal served together," I explain. Neither Connal nor I elaborate on Connal and Jake's habit of sharing a woman between them. I've heard they don't cross swords, but none of my business if they do.

After we clear the table for her, she sets out a plate of cookies over on the coffee table and we move our drinks over there. I frown as I notice her wrapping up cookies for Connal to take with him, also.

Jesus, my Brothers will be stopping by every night at dinner time if word gets around. For the next hour, the three of us sit around exchanging stories. Connal finally uses the bathroom and collects the food containers Riley is sending with him.

He looks over at her, “We good?”

She wraps her arms around my waist and nodding, says, “All good. See ya soon, Connal. And Jake is welcome next time also. Maybe Monday again?” Calling out his thanks, he heads out.

“What was that about?” I ask, looking down at her.

“I’ll tell you all about my day after you make me come at least twice!”

CHAPTER TWENTY-TWO

GUNNER

Laughing, I throw her over my shoulder and head to the bed, spanking her round ass as I go. "Someone's getting greedy!"

"Are you complaining?!" Is the muffled reply, as she sticks her hand down the back of my jeans, pinching my ass.

Putting her down, we both shed our clothes and I grab a condom from my stash inside the closet.

"On your hands and knees, right now," I call out. My Sweetheart is always so quick to comply. When I get on the bed behind her, I decide that the wall next to the bed would be greatly enhanced with a mirror. God, the thought of watching her tits bounce while in this position almost makes me come before I enter her.

Reaching forward, I gather her hair into one hand, pulling her head back. "Tell me what you want, Sweetheart."

"You, Gunner. All of you." She moans as I reach around to squeeze her nipples, not letting up my grip on her hair. I slowly grind my cock along her lower lips feeling her moisture build. Pulling back, I spank her twice on each side.

"Be explicit. What you want, where you want it, how fast or slow, how you feel. You stop telling me, I stop giving it to you," I instruct.

"Gunner, please!" She actively starts trying to wiggle back to mount my hardness, I pull back and spank her again.

"Behave, I thought you wanted to come tonight?" Keeping my cock away from her tight pussy, I rub the red marks on her ass, impatiently waiting for her surrender.

I feel her shudder before she starts talking. "Your cock, Gunner. I want it all the way up my pussy. Fast, I'll come on your cock so just fuck me as hard as you want." She moans as I enter her. "Harder. Give me more!"

It's like a goddamn floodgate. Once Riley starts, she just keeps on as if I would have the control to stop. I was hitting her cervix by the time she said 'up' and I go full speed, not taking it easy on her as I have over the past week.

"Play with your clit!" I order, unable to keep the roughness from my voice. All the while she is trying to complete sentences until she comes. Her tunnel rippling along my dick, as though acknowledging the pleasure I gave her.

I continue on, holding her hips and mercilessly pounding into her as the upper half of her body sinks down unable to support her weight anymore. I finish, filling the condom but I'm not done. She's only come once. Removing the condom, tying it off and tossing it off the bed, I flip her over and worship her pretty cunt with my mouth.

I start by lapping up the juices from her first orgasm, the taste is more intoxicating than the whiskey I had over dinner. Sliding my tongue from inside her pussy up to her clit brings forth a low cry from Riley, the first sign of life since she came and I grin up at her before getting back to business on her sweet spot.

Finishing her off a second time, she tugs my body up alongside her and gives me her mouth. Knowing she is freely sucking her juices from my mouth makes me hard again. Tapping down on that, I won't take her a second time tonight. I want to make sure my sweet Riley recovers from the pounding she just took.

"Gunner?" She whispers.

"I didn't hurt you, did I, Ri?" I murmur into her hair.

"No, Gunner. I just want to get a mirror for that wall. So I can see you next time." I can't help but laugh, my sweetheart is just as dirty as her man.

"I was thinking the same thing. You do that, I'll get the grill for the deck."

"And we need to talk." Fuck, that's just never what a guy wants to hear. My half-hard cock instantly softens.

Leaning over, I pull the blanket over us and settle in as she catches me up on her day. While my instincts and experience tell me to handle it, I know her Gram has a plan to deal with Riley's parents. The threat of any type of restraining order will go a lot further towards stopping Kennelly and slowing down her parents, rather than my preferred method.

We discuss scenarios and decide to put that on hold for now. The next thing I want to know, "Did Connal say something to you? What was that when he was leaving?"

"He's looking out for you," she says shyly.

"Riley, what did he say? I know Flint upset you and I want to know what Connal said."

Repeating it back to me, I relax a bit. In the talks we've had, the one thing I'm certain of is that Riley is a 'when the going gets tough, the tough get going' kind of girl. Then she starts giggling and buries her face in a pillow.

"Sweetheart?"

"Nothing, just something I said to him. I let him know I know life won't always be perfect. But what he doesn't know is, my life has never been perfect. Until this past week," she says while placing soft kisses on my various tattoos.

My arms are still tight around her when I wake up right before dawn. Getting out of bed, I step on the goddamn condom from last night and fuck-all, get my jizz everywhere.

Hopping to the bathroom, I try to clean myself off without waking Riley. Sneaking back, I throw a towel over the mess on the floor and head to the front room to make a call.

Ronnie, the rent-a-cop I know at the university, picks up on the third ring. "Yeah?"

"I need you to ask around about something for me," I start, then explain about Kennelly.

We hang up shortly afterwards and I know even if it isn't Kennelly, I'll have a good description by noon. I've also given him permission to call the sheriff to verify that Kennelly's been temporarily suspended, not that he will.

RILEY

I head to school early, needing to stop at Security to get information on who may have been asking around for me yesterday. As suspected it was Kennelly. I provide Sheriff Michael's phone number to the head of the security department so he can confirm that Kennelly has already been reprimanded for harassing me.

Taking this more seriously than I expected, the security officer then promises me a statement from the person who let Kennelly on campus the day before. At my puzzled look, he explains that his daughter was stalked and nearly raped at a university upstate. The head of security there knew the attacker and didn't pay much attention to the girl's concerns. I nearly cry in relief but also for the terror this unknown girl faced. I will let Gunner know, but by now I'm pissed and happy to let Gram's lawyer follow through.

After class, I am really excited to meet Kristy for lunch. We sit at a smaller table although several people had waved to her. It was really nice to have one on one time with her, and though she mentions upcoming parties with an open attitude, I shy away from that but tell her that she has to come check out my place and Rowansville sometime.

Hearing her bluntly talk about her last two hook-ups get me so embarrassed. Her encounters are nothing like what I've had, I know she thinks I don't share mine because I'm less experienced. But while I don't have her numbers, I can't imagine not coming with Gunner.

As we're leaving, I notice an email from the school's security department and quickly forward on the statement. I want my Gram's lawyer to have hard evidence about Kennelly flashing his badge and telling the guard that he was there on official business.

CHAPTER TWENTY-THREE

RILEY

After classes and the library, I head to Gunner's shop. The door is locked but he opens it quickly after I knock, the warmth of his body chasing away the chill of the outdoors.

"Didn't expect you, Sweetheart! Everything alright?" He asks in between kisses.

"Uh-huh. Just have more reading to do but with the storm warning, I wanted to leave campus earlier than planned. Thought I'd read here and watch you work," I say while I kiss his neck and nibble on his earlobe.

"Don't mind the distraction one bit!" He leads me in and explains the specially ordered piece he's working on.

I explain about my earlier meeting on campus and about the report I received. He basically shrugs it off but starts focusing on my breasts, instantly turning me to putty. He quickly slides my sweater and bra up out of his way. So much for reading here...

Moving his hands away, I kneel in front of him. Rubbing my face against his crotch while I work to unfasten his belt and jeans, I eventually pull his cock through the slit in his briefs. Sucking him into my mouth, I get very enthusiastic as he hardens with my tongue working around his wide cock.

As Gunner slowly works to thrust more and more of his length into my mouth and throat, we are completely oblivious to the change in the background noise. The door is not only open but when I take a breath and focus my eyes, three men are standing there. I fling myself off of him and behind the closest piece of furniture. My freak out causes Gunner to swear and look around, grabbing his fully extended cock.

Three of us are calling out some version of 'Shit', 'Oh my God', or 'Fuck,' while Hawk calmly says, "Hey Riley, nice to see you again," as he closes the door behind him.

Gunner moves to pick me up and quickly carries me towards the back room, knowing how mortified I am. He coos into my ear and places me on the old sofa, working to get his package back in his pants.

"Gunner, I..." I stop, not even knowing what to say and too horrified to consider facing them.

"The two you don't know are Jasper and Vice. Take a couple minutes but you'll have to face them eventually." He drops a kiss on my forehead, heading towards the main room. He veers suddenly towards the kitchenette. Pouring a finger of whiskey and delivering it to me, he heads out to meet his Brothers.

I look at the drink a moment then shoot it. Knowing my face is still bright red, I adjust my bra and sweater and follow Gunner back out to the main room. The men continue talking as I approach. Gunner reaches a hand out toward me and I focus on that, knowing the others are watching me.

He pulls me into his side, drops another kiss on my forehead before replying to a question from the shorter man standing next to Hawk. I gradually study the three invaders.

Hawk gives me a small nod before looking quickly back to Gunner. The shorter of the other two keeps his eyes on Gunner, though from the twitch of his mouth I know he's aware of my gaze. The tallest of the three is close to Gunner's height but only carries about half his weight. His eyes are assessing me, unblinking. The darkest eyes I've ever seen.

I work to meet his stare unblinking and I quickly realize the look isn't unkind, just curious. I know without being told this is Jasper. When their discussion pauses, I move forward with my hand out.

"Jasper? I'm Riley. Believe it or not, I've had more embarrassing days, not by much mind you," I quip with some whiskey courage in me.

The shorter man snorts at my comment, "Vice?" Jasper hasn't taken my hand so I drop it, just nodding at Vice.

"Hi, Hawk. How is Anne?" I ask, hoping for a reply from one of these men.

"She's good, I'll tell her you still have her earrings on." He smiles back at me.

I step back until I'm met with Gunner's chest and he puts a hand on each of my shoulders.

Jasper looks over my head at Gunner. "Flint said he'll back your claim when you make it. Are you sure?" I shift between either foot, wanting to kick this man who won't acknowledge me.

"She's mine. I've told you, I'm not letting her go," Gunner firmly states. Jasper finally looks back at me and I'm too annoyed to blink or look away. Moments pass until he finally nods his head. He turns to leave and the other two follow him. "Welcome to the club, little girl," he calls over his shoulder.

We stand there even after the door has been closed behind them. I finally step away from Gunner, turning, "What the fuckballs, Gunner?"

"Fuckballs?" He tilts his head, smirking at me.

"Gunner!"

"Riley, Jasper was going *old school.* He knows, whether he's thrilled or not, that I'm going to claim you. He wasn't going to acknowledge your greeting yet, in case it pissed me off." He fiddles with his cock through his jeans and continues, trying to suppress a grin. "Vice is kind of a talker, so others will hear about this."

"Can you take me there sometime? The clubhouse?" I don't know why I feel the need to specify. I just know that everyone's hesitancy about who I am is not going to go away if I don't have the opportunity to get to know the men he calls his Brothers. "Me, spending time there might help?"

"You're right, I meant to do it sooner, I just like having you to myself," he says after staring at me a moment. "Maybe in a night or two, let me get Bree to be there, okay?" Stepping towards me and smiling at me, "Now, where were we?"

"Keep it in your pants, Gunner! That door is unlocked!" I jump away from him, laughing as I hightail it to the door. I call back "See you at home!"

Turning to blow him a kiss, my big, scary giant pretends to catch it and plant it on his cheek. "I'll be there in an hour. Let me just finish the sanding here?"

Giggling, I get into my truck, my embarrassment already a faded memory.

GUNNER

Locking up an hour later, I text Riley to let her know I'm heading home. I've already reached out to Bree and Connal. They'll all be at the clubhouse the next night. That'll be a nice group to get Riley comfortable. With Ol' Ladies present, the Girlies generally move parties to the back rooms, so that shouldn't be too much of a problem.

I've been able to get a good amount of inventory built up and am going to discuss the possibility of the store with Flint and Jasper the next day. I know Jas is still dealing with the embezzlement issue, but I want to get his read on it.

Frowning that Riley hasn't texted me back, my next call is to Hawk. I start to run the idea of a store past him but he quickly mumbles something about the boss and hands the phone to Anne. She is interested in further formulating the plan and will talk to Danna, the third person I had thought to include. I try not to get too excited, but this just might work.

I walk into a nearly dark apartment with the sound of Riley's raised voice coming from the bedroom. Following that down the hall, I enter the bedroom to find her pacing. Phone in hand.

"Mother, that simply isn't true." Seeing me, she points to the bed. I sit on the end and am momentarily surprised when she curls up on my lap. I pull her into me, hiding my grin. Placing my chin on the top of her head, I'm so pleased she finds comfort in my presence as I do hers, that I barely pay attention to her conversation.

Until she exclaims, "For the love of God!" Looking up at me, "Gunner, are you grooming me for a sex ring or to be a mule? Mother isn't sure which, but apparently it's one of the two!"

Rolling my eyes, “Neither, I’m keeping you all to myself and out of trouble.” I reply in a voice loud enough to be heard, given my proximity to the phone.

“I didn’t lie, he wasn’t here and now he is. Why would it even matter if he’s with me or not?” She asks, giving me a bad feeling. It would only matter if someone were coming to get Riley and wanted her alone. “Whatever, enjoy Boise.”

Riley pitches the phone over my shoulder and turns to straddle me. She starts relaying the conversation, one that lasted nearly ten minutes but got nowhere.

“Sweetheart, when she first called, did she ask if you were alone?” I ask her softly.

“What?” She’s started nuzzling my neck. “Oh, yeah, she asked if you were here. The whole conversation was weird. I don’t think we’ve ever talked that long.”

Getting up, I place her on the bed, moving to the gun nook I built into my side of the bed frame. I put my Glock in the back of my jeans and go to check that the doors are locked. Looking out the front window, I’m relieved to see a fairly empty street.

“You think they were going to try to take me, don’t you?” I can barely hear her voice though she’s not more than ten feet behind me.

“Sweetheart, I don’t know that.”

RILEY

I don’t even know what to say at this point. I turn back to the bedroom and quickly get into bed, hugging a pillow to my chest.

“Hey, Sweetheart, it’s going to be alright.” Gunner has followed me back and slides in behind me. Turning into him, I worry about how much more of my family drama he can stand. He continues to rub my back, telling me about going to the MC bar the next night to hang out a bit. I smile, hardly distracted, but happy that I'll see Bree again.

Moving closer into him, I notice him shifting away from me. And remember the unfinished business from earlier. Grinning to myself and not saying anything, I keep moving into him and he moves back, unaware that I'm in slow pursuit of the object that he seems determined not to share with me as he continues to soothe me.

A giggle finally escapes me and he draws back from me, frowning. "Something funny, Sweetheart?"

I start laughing and he starts growling at me. "I'm trying to make you feel better, dammit!"

"Why don't you make us both feel better, Gunner?" I coo.

"Be careful what you wish for Riley." He rolls off the bed, removing his clothes and telling me to do the same. After I do, I lay back, spreading my legs for him, frowning as he moves towards the bathroom. "Picked this up for you the other day," he comes out rubbing something all over his cock. "Get that ass in the air, Sweetheart. I'm making that tight, little hole mine tonight."

CHAPTER TWENTY-FOUR

RILEY

I LAY THERE GAPING AT HIM AS HE TOSSES THE BOTTLE OF LUBE on the bed beside me. "Gunner?"

"Who do you belong to, Riley?" He glares down at me. "Gonna make sure you feel me all over."

I roll onto my stomach, pushing up onto spread knees, showing him what he's determined to take. Reaching over, he sticks his finger first into my damp pussy, sliding that juice up towards my other hole, he slowly works the rim. Taking the bottle he pours out more lube, steadily working his finger up inside me.

"It'll hurt a bit at first, Sweetheart. Take deep breaths and push out when I go in," he whispers tenderly. "Just trust me, ok? I'll always make sure you feel good."

Getting behind me, he starts grinding his cock along my lower lips, repeatedly hitting my clit with its head. That stimulates me along with the steady motion of his finger in my virgin hole, making me wetter and wetter, getting me excited for what's to come.

"Gunner?" I pant.

"What, Sweetheart?"

If anything, I've learned how explicit he likes me to be in bed. "Fuck my ass with your big dick, please? It belongs to you and you haven't had it yet."

Letting out a deep, ragged breath, Gunner pulls his finger out and quickly replaces it with the head of his cock. His first push feels like it will rip me apart and only makes it just inside my tight ring, easing further he's soon halfway inside me. Slowly, he rocks himself until his whole length is in me while I try to relax, exhaling.

"That's my girl, that's my tight fucking girl! Tell me whose dick you ride?" With the pain of my body only starting to lessen, he's barely making sense to me. I scream out as he rubs my clit before he gradually pumps faster into my tightest hole.

"Gunner. Just you. Just your cock, in any of my holes. Oh God, I'm going to come!"

"That's it, Sweetheart, strangle my fucking dick in this tight ass of yours." The friction increases as he nears his release; the initial pain I had felt has turned to pleasure and my body is taut with the need to come.

Suddenly, he pinches my clit and my release is upon me. I feel it in every inch of my body as it overwhelms me and the tightening of my anal muscles pull Gunner to his ending. I feel the warm gush of his release way up inside of me before I sink down in a daze.

He collapses on top of me, rolling us to our sides. We are panting, our breathing in sync with each other and I doubt he's any more in control of his limbs right now than I am.

Laying there some minutes, he slides his body over mine, cupping my face in his large, calloused hands. "I love you. Every inch of you. You're everything I need and want. Stick with me, Riley?"

My giant is showing me his weakness, his fear he'll scare me away. "Always," I promise.

"I want to give you everything. You have all of me, but anything you need, ask." Gunner's arms tighten around me and he seems frantic in his desire to please me.

Wrapping myself around him, I kiss the line of his scar and reassure him. "You are what I want, you are what I need."

"Always, Riley. You'll always have me, but I can't lose you. I need you so bad," he vows before claiming my mouth with his.

No fancy dinner that night, Gunner leaves bed shortly to make us sandwiches. We eat, talk, and cuddle, so content to be naked in each other's arms. Before sleep overtakes us, he quietly gets a condom, looking at me for permission before sliding it on. He makes love to me so gently, even when I squeeze my feet into his flanks and ask him for more. He just takes his time while cupping my face and staring down into my eyes. We come together long minutes later and, as always, he cleans me when we finish.

GUNNER

Riley drifts off to sleep in my arms. I love to watch her. No cares or concerns on her face, her innocence radiant. She burrows deeper into me anytime I shift, and this simple movement means as much to me as her professions of love.

CHAPTER TWENTY-FIVE

GUNNER

TODAY HAS BEEN A CLUSTER FUCK. NEITHER RILEY NOR I HAD set our alarms and so we had to race out the door once we finally woke up. I had to continue looking into the list of suspects who may have stolen from the Club. Thankfully, Wrench has been cleared so he's able to do whatever the fuck he does online and can help.

Not the part of my job I enjoy, investigating and suspecting the worst of my Brothers. Granted, with any group, there'll always be the ones you don't like but you still have to trust them to have your back when shit gets real. Investigating them behind their backs tilts the whole balance.

I get home later than planned and nearly shit myself as Riley exits the bedroom. She's beautiful without trying but tonight she's dressed up, her hair is blown out, and it's the first time I've seen her in makeup. She wears it very lightly, but I know her well enough to know it's there. Her eyes are subtlety highlighted and she has a light lip gloss on. She's wearing tight jeans, knee-high black leather boots, and a long sleeve, see-through, dark blue blouse with a camisole underneath.

"Fuck, Sweetheart."

"Is that good or bad?" She smiles at me, fishing for compliments.

"You are stunning." I might have to claim her tonight. Depending on the crowd, some of those motherfuckers will be trying for a piece of her. "Do you want to stay home?"

She narrows her eyes at me, so I throw her a smile to pretend that I'm not trying to keep her here and all to myself. "Are we riding your bike?"

"Yeah, weather's not bad. Let me shower, I'll be ready in ten." As promised I'm back to her in a short while and she's just finishing wrapping up a few food containers. "What's that, Riley?

"Oh, Connal texted me asking for more cookies since we were meeting them tonight. I didn't know if we were going in the truck or bike so I'm just wrapping them now. This'll fit in the bag, won't it?"

"Fuck, you look so amazing I didn't notice the smell," I say, putting her on the counter and giving her my best glare. "Sweetheart, I thought we decided that all your cookies are for me? Now I'm going to have to fucking kill my Brother for trying to get what's mine."

She laughs at me and leans up to kiss my freshly shaved chin. I swear I make grown men wet their pants with that glare.

"Baby? We aren't talking about my cooo-kiesss," she says in an adorable sing-song voice. "Don't get possessive over plain old cookies. Come on, I'm excited, can you carry the containers?" She slides down from the counter, giving my cock a squeeze before escaping my arms. I'm left shaking my head and adjusting my hardening dick inside my jeans.

It's cold out for the ride, but I keep gloves for her in my saddlebag now, and really, the cold just makes her hold me tighter.

I pull up next to Connal and Jake's bikes, secure our helmets and get the cookies out, handing them to Riley to carry. I'm still giving her a hard time about what's mine as we enter. Pretty full room. Brothers turn to look and greet me as I entered first, not the gentlemanly thing to do, but I was hoping to shield Riley a bit.

As I slip my hand from hers to secure it around her waist, silence spreads through the crowd, starting close to us and moving back as others turn to get a look at my Riley. Vice is at the bar and walks quickly towards us.

"You are one lucky son of a bitch, Gunner!" He smiles and slaps me on the back before turning to wink at Riley. "Nice to see you again, sorry to catch you unaware the other day." He smirks at her.

From the barely disguised leers and laughs around us, Vice didn't waste a moment telling them about the interrupted blow job in the shop. Ri's face flames red, but my girl doesn't run.

"I think you should be apologizing to Gunner, not me." She smiles up at me and I see the nervousness but resolve in her eyes. Vice lets out a bark of surprise at her answer.

"Guessing you made it up to him anyway, didn't ya?" Slurs Needle from the bar. Riley rolls her eyes and holds tight to my side when I start to talk to him about his mouth.

"Hey, Riley! Move aside, Gunner, I need my fix!" Connal makes it through the crowd, rubbing his hands together and giving her the biggest puppy dog eyes, "Did you bring them, Riley?"

She holds out the containers of cookies. "I wrapped the batches separately," she narrows her eyes at him. "You said you were going share them? But I figured you'd want some for later."

"I would pledge myself to you, but Gunner already looks pissed." Connal's an observant fucker.

"Yes! He wants all my cooo-kiesss for himself," she replies in a mock whisper. I start growling, as the nosy motherfuckers around us are hanging on every word exchanged.

"Oh, Gunner, there's Bree!" Riley smiles towards the table just past the bar. Taking the chance, I tug her hand and, glaring at everyone in range. We head back towards Flint, Bree, and Jake. Jake stands at our approach and gets introduced, giving Riley and me his trademark nod. He generally doesn't talk much and doesn't say a word as we all sit around talking. Connal reemerges with just one of the containers of cookies and opens it for the table.

Trying them, Bree and Flint quickly compliment Riley, while Jake goes so far as to smile at her. Bree, sitting next to Riley, quickly starts giving her a discrete rundown of the men in the room. It being a school night, most of the other Ol' Ladies are home with their children. Deb and the other Girlies are scattered throughout the room along with Anne's sister and a couple other women I've never seen before.

As I nurse my drink, I'm half paying attention to Connal and Flint, but mostly watching Riley. She's so fucking beautiful, from the looks she's getting it has not gone unnoticed around here either. I release her hand to grab one of the cookies in front of us and she quickly looks over, then she firmly plants her hand high on my thigh. Fuck, yeah.

Vice wanders over and as he looks for a chair to drag up to our table, I simply scoop my girl up and settle her on my lap. I love that her squeal attracts the attention of those who have been eyeing her. Bree quickly slides into her vacant seat so Vice can sit next to Flint.

"God! These cookies are great!" Vice enthusiastically announces as he goes for two more. Smiling over at Riley who has curled into me, "I see why Gunner doesn't want to share, but seriously, you two are like Beauty and The Beast. What the fuck is that all about, little girl?"

Grinning down at her, the insult on my lips is cut off by Connal. "Shit, Vice. Don't scare her off! She's having Jake and me over next week and I'll fucking die if I don't get to try her enchiladas."

"You cook, too?" Bree looks up interested.

"I learned growing up. I just hadn't ever cooked for anyone before Gunner and Connal the other night. They said the lasagna was good," she answers shyly, looking back to me for confirmation.

"No, Riley, it wasn't good," Connal is holding his stomach now. "It was hands down the best meal I ever had." My Sweetheart turns all red, as the group look between Connal and her.

I lift her chin to kiss her gently. "It really was," I whisper against her lips. She wiggles her butt against my hard-on as she leans up for another, hungrier kiss and I'm about to carry her back to my old room before Vice interrupts.

"Well, not to invite myself, but what night are we having enchiladas, Riley?" He winks at her.

I growl and drawback to glare at him as Riley remembers her surroundings, her eyes still half-mast with her passion. "Monday." Fuck, why'd she have to go and tell him? "Bree and Flint you're welcome also. I'll get the groceries, but please bring what you'd like to drink since I'm not old enough to buy that." She laughs and tilts her beer at everyone, finishing it off.

Sighing, I slip her off of my lap to go get us all a round of drinks, Jake holds a hand to block his eyes when I stand up, my stiffy nearly at his eye level. Using his allotment of words for the night. "Shit, Man! No one wants to see that."

I jokingly move to shake it near his head. "Fucker."

"They're all just horny teenagers, Riley," Bree says, forgetting my girl is a teenager. I grin while walking away.

"Ha!" Riley laughs, "Me too!" Making everyone laugh.

Although our table is close to the bar, I'm getting either pats on the back or shit about Riley from everyone I pass so it takes a while to get up to it. Still exchanging barbs with those around me, I don't notice Deb's approach until her fingers are curling around the bulge in my jeans.

"Get the fuck off, Deb!" I've had enough of her shit especially after hearing she slapped Betsy last week.

"That's right, Gunner, let me get you off like I used to! I know just how you like it, Honey." She tries to wrap her arms around mine. "I know she can't do you like I do." Fuck, now all eyes are back on me for the second time tonight.

"Where you getting this crap from, Deb? Can't remember saying anything to you other than bend over, 'suck it', or 'get out'." I growl at her, so fucking pissed she won't let this go. She's fucked most the guys here so her obsession doesn't make sense to me. "Disrespect my woman or me again, and you'll be hearing 'get out' one last time."

She stands there with her fists balled up as I turn to the bar, but keep alert for her next move.

"Ahhh, Babycakes, come take a spin on my dick," Frank interjects, putting an arm around her. "I'll make you feel all better."

"Get the fuck off me!" She screams, pushing him back.

Not a smart move, that proud bastard will look for a way to take it out on her ass later. She storms towards the door but seems to realize that she may not be welcomed back if she leaves, so she veers into a group of guys off to the side.

RILEY

As Gunner heads for drinks I excuse myself to find the bathroom, following Bree's pointed finger. Dodging away from a few stray hands on the way, I walk through the door that has a woman with impossibly large tits outlined on it.

Entering the first stall, two women soon enter the bathroom talking.

"Don't worry about it for a second, Shelly!" Is the first thing I hear, "I'm sure he's just wiping his dick on her to embarrass her family."

"I know! That's the only explanation I can think of. I mean everyone knows he doesn't stick his dick in the same girl twice, can't wait to see that Maddock bitch taken down a peg though." Comes the second high-pitched voice.

Finishing up, I head out to face the two loudmouths. They both have about ten years on me, and one bears a strong resemblance to Anne, Hawk's Ol' Lady.

She's smirking at me like I have something to be ashamed of, I move to wash my hands and as I keep silent they both start to laugh. Reaching for the door, I turn back to them.

"Aren't you both a little old to be acting so immaturely?" I ask looking at the first one, turning to the other one, I unwisely continue with, "Maybe that's why Gunner didn't bother sticking his dick in you a second time?"

Spinning on my heel as I leave the bathroom, I connect solidly with a man's chest. Looking up, I'm relieved to see

Jasper, just as the two women have re-opened the door and are reaching out to me.

"Riley. Good to see you here." He's talking to me but glaring at the women behind me.

"Hi, Jasper. Thanks." I fumble hoping it doesn't look like I was running.

Looking down at me, he smiles and raises an eyebrow. I try to look completely innocent, as I shrug my shoulders.

Shaking his head, his smile still in place, "I think Gunner's worried about you, little girl. He invited Emma and me to your apartment for dinner on Monday. Nice that you two could get it furnished already."

He's back to staring down the women at my back while giving them the message that Gunner and I are nesting. Stepping to the side, he lets me pass. I look over my shoulder to see the women retreating back inside the bathroom.

"Great, I can't wait to meet Emma," I call out as I head back to our table. Passing Frank at a different table, he makes a comment to me that is swallowed by the background noise, but his group all laugh.

Reaching our table, I see everyone has been watching for my approach. Gunner is frowning and Bree looks to be on edge. "Everything alright?" He asks as I head straight for my spot on his lap. Nodding, I curl into my regular position and smile at the concerned look on Bree's face.

"I'll go with you next time, Riley," Bree says, "I just wasn't thinking."

Gunner lifts my face to peer down and checks to see if I'm really alright. "Bree, I'm fine. I can manage going to the bathroom by myself." I say as much to him as to her.

Putting his finger over my lips, "Shh, she's right, Sweetheart. You do need to be protected." He looks concerned and

I remember what he said about the first time I came here. It's best to wait to tell him about the bathroom incident, knowing I should before he hears about it elsewhere.

Deciding that distracting him is my best way out of the conversation, I part my lips and dart my tongue out to lick his finger. His eyes widen and he grabs my hips and grinds his rapidly hardening cock into me, leaning down to my ear he licks the shell and whispers, "Don't fucking play with me right now, Riley."

"Hey, Sexy, come dance with me," someone slurs out almost the same second that I register another hand on my back. Jake instantly stands up to move some guy away, I don't hear a word spoken but the guy throws his hands up in a frustrated motion and backs off.

"Fuck this." Gunner snarls looking wildly around him, and I cup either side of his face with my hands. "Fuck this shit."

"What's wrong?" I can't figure out what's gotten in to him, he's suddenly so tense I'm worried for him. Looking down at me, he exhales and leans his forehead up against mine for a long moment before looking up at Flint.

"Is Jasper still here?"

Flint's eyes widen, but he nods and points behind us. Lifting and holding me close as he stands, Gunner turns until he sees Jasper against a back wall talking to another man.

CHAPTER TWENTY-SIX

RILEY

"JASPER!" GUNNER CALLS OUT, LOUD ENOUGH TO SILENCE most of the room.

"Got something you want to say, Brother?" Jasper calls back, grinning at us.

"President, I'm claiming this woman. Riley's my Ol' Lady." Oh. Shit. Tonight? Isn't tonight too soon? My heart starts thumping and I'm sure he can hear it. He squeezes me tight and still has his eyes locked on Jasper.

Jasper finally nods, "I got no problem with that. Any Brothers have any objections to Riley Maddock, speak up now."

Silence. Except for my heart beat, it's so loud I feel like there's a speaker hooked up to it.

"Done," Jasper finally says, turning back to the man at his side.

Gunner just stands there with me still in his arms, as the men around us yell out different forms of congratulations.

Putting my arms around his neck I pull myself upwards and shift to wrap my legs around his waist.

"Gunner?" He jerks his head down to look at me. I rock up to whisper in his ear, "Baby? You haven't fucked me on the couch yet." Horny teenager indeed.

He crashes his mouth down onto mine until I tug his ear, hoping to get some fresh oxygen into my lungs. He scoops up our jackets and starts walking towards the door, I wave at our table over his shoulder. Bree and Flint are whispering to each other, Connal and Vice are laughing at Gunner's antics, while a serious looking Jake waves his hand once at me.

I keep my chin on Gunner's shoulder and legs tight around him, halfway out the door I get a glimpse of a furious looking woman reenacting the phrase 'if looks could kill'.

He helps me into my jacket and onto his bike, getting us home without another word. Carrying me upstairs, he moves straight for the couch.

Oddly, our clothes are still on.

GUNNER

I've been trying to figure out what to say to her the whole way here. I just felt so damn powerless, all their comments, then that jag-off touched her? Fuck, she doesn't even know about the scene with Deb. I pull my hands back to see they are shaking.

"Gunner?" Shit, why does she sound like that? "Gunner, do you want to take it back? Is that it?"

"Goddammit! NO, Riley!" I yell loudly, surprising us both.

She's looking at me with unshed tears in her beautiful

eyes and I'm even more furious at myself. "Riley, we never spoke about any timing with us. I backed you into this corner and you, shit, we've only been together a short time. What do *you* want, Riley? Tell me and I'll make it right."

"Gunner. Everyday we've been together, you have shown me, told me, and proven to me that we belong to each other. You already claimed my heart, mind, and body. Why do you think I care that you announced it to your MC? I mean you told the freaking sheriff you were going to marry me, for Pete's sake!" Her voice got consistently louder as she continued and when she mentions the sheriff, I can see her point. I crush her to me until I hear a joint crack, reminding me to lighten my hold a little.

"I don't have a ring for you yet, Sweetheart," I say, quietly.

"We have time, Gunner." She leans in to kiss me. "I'm not going anywhere."

"Wait. There's this Girlie, I have to tell you about." She tenses up instantly.

"Deb?" She whispers, God only knows what she's heard. "Did...do you love her?"

"Fuck no! Jesus, Riley. I've never loved another woman." Kissing her gently, "She just always made herself available to me, I never encouraged it and didn't even notice I had, ya know, been with her more often than some of the others. Jasper pulled me aside the night he claimed Emma, told me Deb had been telling the other Girlies that she was going to be my Property, my Ol' Lady."

Frustrated but worried over how stiff my Sweetheart is, I hastily finish. "Look, after that I avoided her, and then I met you. I swear it's been over a year since I touched her. It's just tonight, when I went up to the bar, she came up and grabbed that hard-on I was sporting from you squirming on my lap and made a scene. I told her she would be kicked out if she disrespected either of us again."

"I think she was the one who looked like she wanted to kill me when we were heading out? Near the door?"

"I told you I wouldn't apologize for my past, and I was no fucking saint. I just don't want that to hurt you now." I'll never understand this woman. Tears flood and overwhelm her eyes. I did that to her, yet she wraps her arms around me, kissing my neck.

"Two others followed me in to the bathroom," she whispers into my ear. "I think one woman was Anne's sister? Anne had told me that you and she had hooked up a while back. They wanted to stir the pot a bit, but I turned it back on them and ran. Well, Jasper was walking by the bathroom, otherwise they may have tried to beat me down." My little tiger is smiling into my neck, gently hiccupping and wetting down my shirt and cut with her silent tears.

"I love you so much, Sweetheart." I try to hold her tight but she pushes away. Standing in front of me, she removes her blouse, leaving her camisole. Next she sits on the coffee table and starts to remove her boots, but I reach over to help her, pulling each one off. As she slides out of her jeans, I see my Sweetheart went commando tonight! What a nice surprise. "Riley, I can't wait to have you raw again. Felt so fucking good to be in you like that."

She straddles my lap, "We have to give the pill a couple more weeks then that's the only way I want you in me."

"I'll give you kids someday, Sweetheart, I promise." I moan, flicking her nipples through her silky top. "But this selfish bastard wants you all to himself for a bit."

"Why are you still dressed?" She tries to lift my shirt but I pull her arms behind her back, holding them with one hand.

"No, no, no. You may have me all wrapped around your pinky, Riley. But this here? This is when you do what I say." I slowly twist her nipple with my free hand, enjoying the sight of her arching into me with her head back. "Going to make you squirt again, you squirt for me then I'll take my clothes off and give you my cock anyway you want it, you understand?" I flick my thumb across her clit and she starts grinding into that digit.

"Yes, Gunner. Anything you want. Please," she moans as I hold her back by her arms while working my belt off. Gonna need both hands to take care of my girl. Getting that off, I make fast work of securing her wrists behind her back with it. Her eyes are blazing into mine.

"That's my Riley. How does this feel now?" I slowly slid my middle finger up her wet slit searching for her G spot, I clamp my thumb back down on her clit just as I find her inner sweet spot. Securing her in place with a grip on her ass, I let her grind down on my fingers, slathering them with her sweet juice.

"My God, Gunner, please, that's it!" I lean forward and suck, first on one, then on her other nipple. Her grinding down on my hand has increased to a frantic pace, slowly withdrawing my finger I slide it up to my mouth to suck on. "So close, please don't stop, need it," she begs. I unwind my belt from around her wrists and bring her up to stand on the couch, her gorgeous cunt right up to my mouth.

"Quench my thirst, Ol' Lady! Give me all that sweetness." Are my last words tonight, as I secure her in position, my hands on her ass cheeks, Riley's hands are flat on the wall behind the couch, supporting herself.

Tilting her pelvis to suit my need to consume all of her, I fuck her sweet pussy with my tongue; just as deep and eagerly as she needs. Sliding a finger up into her and moving my mouth to focus on her engorged clit, rolling it between my tongue and my teeth, Riley's knees give way and she is unknowingly chanting something along the lines of 'yes', 'please', and 'love'.

Then she gives me what I wanted all night. My Sweetheart squirts all over my face. I get as much of that on my tongue as possible, and when she starts moaning for me to stop, I suck up as much of her inner cream as I can get.

Content, I shift her in my arms and carry her to our bed. I put her down long enough to kick off my boots before pulling her into my side. Holding her, I wipe a hand over my face, inhaling her scent. Happy to be marked by the woman snoring in my arms.

RILEY

Waking in the middle of the night, I'm naked and next to Gunner, who's fully dressed. Hmmm, we'll see about that.

After a quick stop in the bathroom, I head to the closet to grab a condom from Gunner's supply. Reaching into the shelf in the dark, I feel a piece of leather beyond the condoms. As I'm reaching for the light, Gunner's voice startles me.

"Why don't you bring that with you so I can give it to you properly?" Gunner clicks on the light near the bed.

Smiling abashedly, I grab the piece of leather and a rubber before making my way back to him. "You promised me something last night, Gunner."

"You came so hard for me, Sweetheart," he reaches for me, having me straddle him as he lies back taking the items I brought from the closet. "I'll give you what you want, but I want you to have this first."

He unfolds the leather to show me a vest, in small letters

on the front it reads PO Gunner, flipping it I see Property of Gunner and the MC's logo on the back. "OH! Bree had a vest like this on last night!"

"I'm pretty goddamn sure it didn't say 'Gunner,' Sweetheart." He smirks at me, "First thing, you gotta stop calling them *vests*. You're my Ol' Lady now, no one will touch you or give you shit with this *cut* on you. Wear my brand on you?" He raises an eyebrow at me in question.

I smile down at him and lift it up, swinging it on. "You mean like this?" Sitting on him, naked except for his cut, I tease the front of it, rubbing my hands over the leather to caress my boobs.

"Fuck, Riley. Fuck." He grabs the open edges, pulling me down to his lips. "That's so goddamn hot." He murmurs when he lets me up for air.

"Get your pants off, Gunner. I'll show you something better," I say, sliding off of him. He wastes no time shucking his pants.

I nudge him further up, so he's leaning back against the headboard. Maneuvering between his legs, he gets a full view of my ass peeking out from the end of my cut.

I start by licking his balls, taking each in my mouth. Stretching my tongue out, I slide it along the underside of his cock while looking straight in his eyes. Wiggling my butt causes his eyes to shift and I take that moment to pop his rapidly hardening cock into my mouth. He groans loudly, rolling his head back and fisting his hands at his sides. I continue bathing his length, sliding him in and out of my mouth to take him as far back as I can. I still have problems with my gag reflex but am eager to improve.

Shifting back from him, I find and slip the rubber into his hand. Once he's got that on, I turn my back on him and though awkward at first, start practicing that reverse cowgirl he showed me the other day. Bracing myself on his knees, I slip one hand down to massage his balls. I work myself up and down his cock as fast as I can, knowing that if his eyes are open they're pointed at his Property of Gunner cut and our bodies joining below it.

"Tell me when you're close, Gunner."

"Rub yourself, Ri," he moans out. "I want you to come."

"Later, Baby, you take care of me later. This is about you." I manage to get out as I try to focus on him and maintain my speed.

Soon I feel his balls tighten in my hand followed by him bellowing, "Now, Riley!"

I get up. Turning to him I grab his cock, rolling the condom off as I rub up and down his shaft. Shrugging the cut off, I aim his cock right at my breasts. His eyes widen in shock as the realization of what I want him to do dawns on him. Just as he grabs his length in his one of his hands and my shoulder in the other, his jizz bursts out of him in long creamy strands all over my neck and chest.

Holding my boobs together and I scoop up some of his cum, sucking it off my finger and grinning at him. Gunner has slumped back against the headboard but lazily reaches a hand up to rub more of his spunk into my chest. "My little Sweetheart is so, so dirty."

Laughing, I slide from the bed. "Want to come wash me?" I wink at him as I lay out my cut on the end of the bed —making sure it didn't get any of his cum on it!—and head to the bathroom naked but for his seed. I'm already under the rain shower by the time he catches up. He turns on another row of shower heads then sits on the bench, staring at me intently.

"I could watch you all day, Riley." He leans forward curving a hand down one side of my body, reverently. His eyes are filled with wonder and lust as I move into his arms. He holds me close, placing soft kisses across my skin until he shuts off the water, wraps me in a towel and carries me back to bed as though I'm the most precious thing on Earth.

The following days go on in a similar pattern. School for me, work and MC business for him, nights are spent exploring each other and figuring out our weird habits.

Friday night, I showed up at Gram's for my weekly dinner, excited that Gunner was going to join us also. Only he never showed. No reply to my texts but I make an excuse to Gram and hope she'll let it slide. Before dessert is served, I sneak off to call him, the call goes straight to voicemail. I try to stay positive but know that I'm not fooling Gram.

I arrive home to a dark house, and still getting Gunner's voicemail, I pull my cut on, leave a note for him on the counter and head to the clubhouse. Pulling up to a closed gate, I see the new probie and a man I've never seen before are standing outside, as I approach them the stranger yells; "No party here tonight, maybe next week, Honey."

The Probie nudges him as I pull back my jacket to show my cut. "I'm sure I'm allowed in..."

"Sorry," The Probie speaks up, "no one's allowed in, don't matter who."

"Then can you get Gunner for me?" I get a shrug in reply.

"Look, don't know who's in there, who's not. No one in or out until Pres allows. Radio fucking silence, so just go back home." I see a Nomad patch on this guy's jacket and while unsure of what that means, probie is obviously following his lead. I reverse out, trying to figure out what to do. I know Bree is working tonight so don't want to bother her nor cause the hassle of going to her bar underage. With a last look back at the clubhouse, I head home.

CHAPTER TWENTY-SEVEN

GUNNER

What a shit show. Took nearly a week, but I got the evidence needed to prove who was skimming the take. Fucking Needle and Deb. Their fate was decided on by the group, now I have to carry it out.

Each one swearing that the other one planned and got it rolling. No help for Needle now regardless, over a lousy ten grand that they probably already snorted. Deb makes it difficult. No one wants to give her a death sentence, but she's got MC ink on her and those ain't going back out the door with her.

We decide fire is the quickest way to deal with Deb's ink. Roy will treat her for a few days afterwards, then she'll get a one-way bus ticket away from here. She hears that and starts blubbering, looking for mercy, talking about other deals Needle's cut himself in on, so I got to go down and break more ribs until he gives that shit up, too. Not only fucking taking money from all our pockets, but he's got a cousin in what's left of the Spiders and he's dealing meth for them in our town.

Big fuck up there. Keeping shit outta this town has always been a priority and he's fucking dealing to the high school behind our backs.

It's nearly four in the morning before I get back to the clubhouse and retrieve my phone from Jasper's office. Riley is upset, but this is the life sometimes. I go out back to get my bike. Approaching the gate, probie waves me down.

"Man, your Ol' Lady was here, looking good in her cut. You know we couldn't let her in or tell her anything. She looked worried, just wanted you to know."

"Thanks for the heads up. My old room is still empty, why don't you crash there when you get a break?" Probie waves his thanks and I head out.

Hoping she reached out to Bree when she couldn't get me, I push the limit trying to get home. Roads are rough this time of year but I still don't think anything of it when her truck isn't out back when I pull under the deck. Heading up the icy stairs and through the bedroom door, I'm surprised to see an empty bed. I follow the light to the front room and freeze. Easily seeing she isn't there, I check the kitchen counter for the spot she leaves me notes, seeing only the one she left before leaving for the clubhouse. My gut twists and palming my phone to call her, I walk back through looking in the still empty second bedroom then going to our bathroom, finally the closet.

Her clothes are either missing or in stages of having been pulled from hangers, what makes me drop to my knees is her cut. It's perfectly laid out in the center of the mess.

Scrolling through my phone, I recheck my messages before trying her again. Heading to the front window, I can see that her truck isn't on the street in front either. Checking her note again, "G – Worried about you, running to the clubhouse. Charge your phone and call me, I'll come right back. Love you, R"

Heading down to my bike, I set my helmet's Bluetooth so I can start calling people from the road. Driving towards Mrs. R's I call Flint first.

"What." He sounds pissed.

"Brother, can you ask Bree if she heard from Riley. She's gone, I...she had tried to reach me earlier." I drive around Mrs. R's house but see no sign of Riley's truck. It's too early to knock there.

"Calm down, I'll wake her and ask. Let me call you back." Flint's voice is low and calm.

Calling probie next, I have him repeat the entire conversation. I can't figure out anything that would have made her run. Thinking that she ran from me sets me off again.

Approaching my shop, my fuel light goes on. There's no sign of her from the outside, and I never gave her a key, so I head next door to Jasper's house. He'll have fuel or a truck I can use.

The porch light comes on as I approach. Turning off my bike and holding my hands up so he can see it's me, Jasper steps out onto the porch.

"What's wrong, Brother?" He asks. Just then Flint calls back, so I hold up a finger.

"Flint, anything?" I ask. "I just rolled into Jasper's."

"No, Bree was working until two. She double checked her phone and never heard from her."

Looking at Jasper, so he can hear this also, "I went home, Riley wasn't there. She couldn't reach me earlier so had run to the clubhouse. Probie and the Nomad turned her away. Probie said she headed back towards town. Her truck wasn't there, closet was ransacked and her cut was laid out on top. Someone fucking took her, I know someone took her."

I'm nearing freak out mode and I see Emma come up behind Jasper. Jasper looks pained as he opens his mouth. I know what he and Flint don't want to say.

"Fuck!" I want to kick myself. "She has a lockbox with some serious cash at home. I cut a hidey hole into the drywall of the closet. I didn't think to look. I don't believe she left me, I sure as hell don't deserve her but she lov...we love each other. I'm low on fuel, can I?" I motion to his truck.

Jasper looks back to Emma, sharing a look before saying. "Come on, I'll drive you back to the apartment. We can check it out."

"Stay in touch," Emma says quietly, looking up at Jasper before he kisses her.

"Jas, I'll meet you both at the apartment. Emma, Bree's up now and worried. Could you use some company?" Flint pipes up from the speakerphone. Jasper's obviously concerned about her and their twins, so he quickly accepts Bree's help. That all worked out, he and I get in his truck.

Pulling out, Jasper takes a deep breath. "You weren't planning on claiming her so soon, were you?" At my grunt, he continues, "I saw the surprise on both your faces when you did it. Have you two argued since then?"

"No. Not even when I told her that Deb grabbed my cock that night. She let me explain. I had told her at the beginning I'd never apologize for what I did before we met."

"Did you two have plans? Before all that shit went down tonight?" He pushes.

"Yeah, dinner at her Gram's. She called and texted me when she was there. She went home, left me a note and showed up looking for me at the clubhouse. Probie said she was wearing her fucking Property cut, Jasper." Looking at the clock again, I internally debate waking Mrs. R. for the tenth time since I got home. "It's got to be her fucking parents."

Just as Jasper's pulling up, I realize I hadn't given him directions to our place. Narrowing my eyes at him, he shrugs and smirks at me. "Flint told me about the talk he had with her. My Sergeant at Arms moves out of the clubhouse, I'm gonna fucking ask where to, you asshole."

As he follows me upstairs, we both check the doors, looking for obvious signs of fuckery. I walk around the island, grabbing the note from the corner of the counter where she left it for me. Handing it to Jasper, we head back to the bedroom.

Along the back wall of the closet, I quickly shift her shoe boxes, seeing no sign that the drywall was moved I pop the panel out of the way. Grabbing the box, while Jasper watches from the doorway, I key in my birthday. It opens to show the money's all there. Jasper lets out a low, "Fuck."

"Now you gonna tell me my Ol' Lady willingly left me? Left the building she owns? And left ten grand behind?" I slam the box shut and shove it into its spot. Picking up Riley's cut, we both turn as Flint calls out from the front room.

"Flint, gotta get on this now. Get Connal and Jake rolling and have them trace the route from the clubhouse to her place slowly. Look for any signs of her truck or an ambush." Jasper greets him, before looking back to me. "Gunner, have you called her grandmother? If not, now's the time."

Flint looks between us, nods, getting on his phone. I make my own call.

"Alex? Why are you calling?" Mrs. R picks up on the second ring.

“I don’t know where Riley is, the closet was made to look like she left.” I pause, “Mrs. R, she’s not with you?”

“Not since dinner when she made some cockamamie excuse for why you weren’t there, then kept going to the bathroom to call you,” she exhales. “Let me call Rogers, can you come here to meet him?”

“Something came up and I couldn’t reach out. She came looking for me though, now I can’t find her. Jasper and Flint are with me.”

“Well, you’ll need those two with you if her parents are responsible,” It reassures me she thinks the Maddocks are behind this also. If for no other reason than Riley won’t be seriously harmed. “Be here in twenty minutes. Like it or not, I’m calling the sheriff about this.” She disconnects before I can say anything.

“Fuck.” Jasper and Flint were talking but look over at me. “Mrs. R wants us to meet her man over there, but she said she’s calling Michaels about this also.”

“Didn’t you say her attorney was filling some paperwork against Kennelly? Do we know if that has gone through?” Flint asks.

“Shit, I forgot about that. Let’s head over to Mrs. R’s to talk.” They both stand there, blocking the door.

“You cool, Gunner?” Jasper asks bringing himself up to his full height, matching mine.

“I’m not fucking cool, Jasper, but I’m getting my Riley back.” I take a step towards him.

Flint, as always, steps in when my temper flares. “No enemies here, Brother.” Looking to me, “Sheriff’s gonna be involved, you gotta stay frosty, Gunner. No threats made, nothing.”

“We’re wasting time. She needs me. Let’s go.” I ground out, opening the door.

ROGERS

Answering Mrs. Riley's call, I quickly walk the three blocks to her home. As she lays out her directives I consider calling her physician. After thirty years in her employ, this is the second time I've seen her look this poorly and she was much younger when her husband unexpectedly passed.

After bringing her tea, I step into the foyer to await her guests. Soon, I'm shaking my head as I watch Gunner approach the door, Flint, and another man in tow. I can't help but wonder about the wisdom of he and young Miss Riley together, but right now I would not want to be the person keeping them apart.

Opening the door before he can ring the bell, I step out into the cold, closing it behind me.

"Mr. Sorenson," they all pause to watch me, "you must keep in mind Mrs. Riley's age. This is a shock to her and while she will move heaven and earth for Miss Riley, as we proceed, I ask that you bring any information obtained to me first. Understand?"

Studying me for a moment, "Is she alright?" He asks.

"Upset, as we all are, but she's in her seventies and it is my job to protect her," I reply. "Now, I won't hold you up any further." I stand back to allow them entry to the home, pleased they all wipe their feet.

Bringing coffee to the parlor, Mrs. Riley is updating them on the notice that was served to Officer Kennelly yesterday and is picking up the phone. "If you all swear you'll stay silent, I will call my daughter with the speaker-phone on." She said this as more of a command than question.

Nods all around precede her dialing the phone.

"Mother?" A sleep wary voice answers. "What is it?"

"I was hoping you could tell me what, exactly, you might have done with Riley?" Mrs. Riley asks in a calm voice that perfectly expresses how irate she is.

"Riley?" Ann Maddock mumbles.

"Yes, I trust your opioid addiction hasn't caused you to forget your daughter's name?" She snaps, releasing information that causes the four of us to look at each other in stunned silence.

"WHAT?!" Well, that certainly got Ann's attention. "How dare you suggest..."

"Save it, Ann. I've been aware of it for many years now. What's important is that Riley is missing..."

"And you don't think to call the police on that scumbag she moved into the apartment you gave her?!" She shrilly replies.

Gunner looks ready to commit murder, and I can't help but wonder if that won't soon happen.

"Alex is anything but, and he's also the one dragging people out of bed searching for her." Mrs. Riley is staring straight at Gunner, silently willing him to stay calm. "What about that husband of yours or an overeager security person, perhaps?"

Just then the doorbell rings, and moments later I usher in the sheriff. He and I announce ourselves so Mrs. Maddock will know that we, at least, are present.

"For the love of God, Mother. Did anyone check our house before you started upsetting the authorities? Maybe she came to her senses and wanted to get away from that criminal? I can just imagine the headline if the local press gets ahold of this!" Ann continues on, alerting us to her main concern in this matter.

"Ann, so help *me* God, if one hair on that girl's head is harmed and I find out you or Bill had any part in this I will make you regret your very existence!" I have never heard Mrs. Riley raise her voice nor seen her hang up on anyone. Until this moment.

Taking a deep breath, Mrs. Riley looks to me. "Rogers, take Gunner and search their house and property, please? You know where the key is."

Gunner goes to Mrs. Riley, whispers in her ear then kisses her cheek. She watches him as he walks from the room, and although I've known they've become close over the years I'm still surprised at the love for him that I see shining from her eyes. Nodding to Mrs. Riley as she notices me watching her, I follow behind him.

Motioning him through the kitchen and picking up the keys we continue on to the garage, getting into one of the trucks as his phone starts ringing.

"Go, Connal." His harsh voice rings out then he's silent for a moment. "Ok, stay where you are, either the sheriff or Flint will be out."

Holding his hand up to stop my question, he dials his phone. "Mrs. R., my guys found a patch of nails near mile marker one forty-seven, looks like a vehicle recently skidded off the road near there. Maybe the sheriff could look into that?" It seems Gunner is willing to let Michaels chase evidence.

Gunner quickly makes another call, all I hear is, "Wrench, call Connal, get the information on the truck that Riley just bought and do what you can to track that down." Click.

"Mr. Sorenson?" He looks at me as if he had forgotten I was here. "Mrs. Riley is quite ill, she's been hiding it for a while now so I do not believe Riley is aware." As the silence stretches on, I continue, "If you'll forgive me for talking out of school?"

"I have thought so too, these past few months. She'd never say anything, though would she?" He finally acknowledges my thoughts. "What do Riley's parents stand to gain from Mrs. R's death, do you know? I would guess there's a trust?"

"There was a sizable trust set up by Mr. Riley. Ann would be next in line for that." I pause, weighing how to balance loyalties. "Let's say, while unnecessary to be used so, the trust has been tapped for Mrs. Riley's living expenses and her charitable expenditures."

"Unnecessarily?" He grunts. "She had other money that could have covered expenses with, but she chose to use the trust?"

"Precisely." I pause again, letting him think about why it was handled that way, allowing me to merely confirm his guesses.

"Because Mrs. R can't stop Ann from inheriting the trust, but she can leave her own money to anyone or thing she damn well chooses?"

Mr. Sorenson catches on quickly. "Indeed."

"So she's been bleeding the trust dry?" He smirks at the thought.

"Don't get me wrong, she's funded childcare centers for working mothers and drug rehab centers with it. However, day to day items and my salary come from the trust instead of her own funds."

"I suppose you're paid quite well?" He raises an eyebrow at me, so I shrug and he continues. "Do Riley's parents have any idea about this?"

"That is, indeed, a worry we have shared for some time," I acknowledge. "She keeps close tabs on them, however, and their spending habits would say otherwise. Ah, here we are now."

GUNNER

Once again I'm left to wonder about the man sitting next to me. He quickly unlocks what looks like an empty house and directs me to the entrance to the basement as he goes upstairs. I make my way down, past a game room and movie theater and into the storage rooms he told me I would find. No one seems to have been down here for a while.

Heading back up, I check the rooms on the main floor with growing impatience. Rogers rejoins me and looking around, I finally realize what I haven't seen in any room.

"There aren't any pictures of Riley here?"

"Who was around to take them, Mr. Sorenson?" He looks at me intently. "Under Mrs. Riley's orders, her nannies started taking some. Mrs. Riley keeps albums at her house including pictures she took, if you're interested in them one day."

"Fucking bullshit," slips out before I can stop myself.

"Exactly my feelings, Mr. Sorenson," Rogers quickly confides.

Next, we walk out through the garage that houses the SUV that Riley's parents reclaimed from her, then a long empty barn.

"The Maddocks' stopped bringing riding parties here on weekends and sold off the horses one day. Miss Riley was ten and so upset, I don't think she's gone near a horse since then," he explains. "I'm not aware of any other buildings on the land. Let me check back in with Mrs. Riley before we go."

Coming up empty here has me furious. Calling Jasper he gives me two addresses to check. "Wrench is searching for property in Kennelly's name. It's a long shot but all we have right now. The sheriff called all the deputies in and he was the only one who didn't respond. No one's seen him since yesterday morning."

"Rogers!" I yell over to him. "It's Kennelly, give me your keys. I'm driving." I'm honestly surprised when he tosses them to me and runs to the passenger side of the Lexus.

Racing to the nearest of the two properties, Rogers and I ride in silence. I control my breathing as I wonder at the man beside me, wondering what Jasper was thinking having him accompany me. Then it hits me. He's here as a witness. A witness in my defense.

I nearly slam on the brakes, but keep going. Thirty minutes later as I'm pulling into the drive, Flint calls.

"Hey, where are you?"

"Just pulling into the first address," I say, slowing down.

"Yeah, I just checked that, it's a bust. Go to the other one Wrench gave you, see that you check around back for an old storm cellar." My nerves are stretched so tight I'm about to snap when I realize it's an open line. They've somehow gotten Riley's location and that's what matters most to me. For now.

Until later, when I will skin the motherfucker that took her alive.

Without another word, I head to the second location. Rogers stays silent.

CHAPTER TWENTY-EIGHT

RILEY

I HAVE NEVER BEEN SO FRIGHTENED IN MY LIFE. A SUDDEN flat sent me flying off to the side of the road, I managed to get control but my cell flew aside and I was still trying to find that when a tow truck pulled up.

I was so relieved until I saw the drivers face. Too late.

I remember Kennelly holding a cloth over my face and saying, "They may have said they won't pay me anymore, but they'll pay well enough to have you away from that big bastard."

I'm not sure how long I've been wherever it is I am. My mouth is gagged, I'm hogtied, and so cold. I've squirmed around enough to see what looks like a duffle bag of mine in one corner but nothing else. There has been a steadily increasing light coming through the boards of the door in the ceiling and that is the only thing keeping me from full out panic.

I don't know where Gunner was the night I was taken. I didn't have any plans the next day, now today. So if he hasn't gotten back no one will know I'm missing and that is the thought that terrifies me.

I've read enough true crime stories to know that the longer I'm gone, the harder it will be to find me. I vary from praying for Gunner to singing songs in my head, anything but thinking about what will happen if no one comes for me. Or worse, if the wrong person comes for me.

My jacket and cut have been removed and thinking that Kennelly ran his hands over me makes me fight back vomit each time the thought pops into my head. Vomiting into this gag would surely cause me to suffocate.

My hands have gone numb and while I've kicked off one shoe, I can't get the ropes to budge. My back is racked with spasms, so I try to take deep breaths. Failing in that, I can no longer fight my fears and begin to sob until I feel nothing else.

What seems like hours later a noise from the door above me doesn't initially register, a loud banging noise, then a crash and light floods the room. A whispered, trembling voice says "Sweetheart?"

I scream through my gag and start to wiggle closer to the staircase.

"Rogers! She's here!" Gunner bellows and I start crying harder than ever. Suddenly his hands are cupping my face and he's saying, "I got you, Sweetheart. Look at me, look at me, ok?" I nod in reply.

"I got to cut this all off, just hold still. Don't move at all." Drawing a knife from his boot, he first cuts my gag off.

My mouth is so dry I can't form words. Then panic retakes me as a shadow blocks the light.

"Rogers, go find some water for our girl, she's in a bad way." Gunner looks up at my gram's right hand. Rogers smiles and nods, then disappears. "Keep your eyes open, we don't know where he is."

"I got you, Riley. I'm so sorry, Sweetheart." Gunner repeats over and over again. My mind is too tired, my throat too dry, I can do nothing but fall limply to the ground as he continues to slice through the ropes holding me, nothing except enjoy the hints of freedom as they come.

Rogers quickly returns, bottle of water in hand. Gunner has Rogers slowly pour that into my mouth as he continues to cut off the pieces of rope wrapped around each of my limbs. Needles stab my hands and feet as the ropes are cut free and circulation returns. Gunner rubs each limb while Rogers continues to drip water into my mouth.

As I get control, my mind grasps one thought. "Gunner, he took my cut off. I lost my cut."

Rogers helps to slide me forward into Gunner's embrace. "Shush, Sweetheart, I have it in the truck. I've got it. Got to get you out of here now, alright?" He says while placing light kisses all over my face.

Walking over to the corner, Rogers looks into the bag. "I think this is hers?"

I nod when they both look at me. After that, all the energy I can muster is used to snuggle my head into Gunner's chest.

Faintly aware of being transferred from arm to arm, I cry out anytime I think I'm away from Gunner. Sometimes he's there to soothe me, other times I feel my gram's hand on my head. Voices always murmur that I'm safe.

FLINT

Fucking went off on my own and ran smack into Kennelly. He was walking away from his brother-in-law's junkyard.

Had that piss ant duct-taped and in the back of my SUV in no time. Called Jasper to meet me at our safe house.

Wrench had already given us properties to check, including one Kennelly had listed under his mother's name. Ten minutes with Jas and me was all it took for Kennelly to give it all up. Called Gunner to point him towards his woman.

Jas and I head back to Mrs. Riley's, while the Nomad stands guard over Kennelly. He is to await Gunner's retribution.

EILEEN RILEY

When my husband died I felt suffocated. My daughter, who we gave everything to, played the devastated child to perfection for our friends and associates. We spoiled her. I knew that, but loved her to bits. She despised us both, and at the time of her father's death held her newborn daughter over me like a Lord.

My disgust at what I had raised caused me to be cautious around Riley. Darling Riley, who never wanted anything other than a hug. By the time she was old enough to see that her parents would never care for her, I was unable to bring her into my household.

I insisted on Friday dinners. Through years of chemo treatments, promises of remission, I put on a brave face. Afraid for the day I wouldn't be there for her.

God does work in mysterious ways. The day came that Alex—Lord, I have to remember he prefers Gunner now—came to me. He'd stumbled upon Riley and somehow knew she was meant to be his. I remember the absolute panic that flooded me with his announcement that day, replaced almost immediately with calm. He told me a dozen reasons why he was wrong for her, but that he wanted to take away all her pain. To treasure her.

I've spent today waiting for word on my granddaughter before Rogers' call finally came. Relief floods me when Gunner comes in carrying our sweet girl. I can only point upstairs, unable to speak.

Rogers grabs my wrist. "I'll call your doctor. I want him to check both of you." Gunner says and I realize I'm no longer running this. "I'm going to collect my gun and will be here when Gunner needs to step out."

Nodding, although it isn't necessary, I head upstairs.

Gunner has laid Riley on the bed in the first room he comes to. I go to get a wet cloth and water glass from the bathroom. Coming out, I see that he has opened her jeans and is trying to gauge if any further damage had been done. I hold the doorframe, swaying, not having considered that atrocity.

Seeing him nod to himself and refasten her pants sets my world right again. He looks back at me like he knows I was watching. "I think she's alright. I don't know for sure, but our girl will get the care she needs."

Our girl indeed.

GUNNER

After the doctor comes and goes, and I'm satisfied with his promise to come back in the morning, I spend the night wrapped around my Sweetheart.

Either waking her from her nightmares or to ease her thirst, I watch over her, apologizing every time I can that there was MC business that kept me from protecting her. Riley's cries, asking me to stay with her, break my heart over and over.

When morning comes, I reverently whisper my devotion to her and explain that I have to leave her here with her gram and Rogers for a while. That I'll check in when I can but knowing that I won't be back before nightfall. Even then, I don't know if my sweet Riley will ever want my hands on her again.

Before I leave, I put the cut that I got her beside her on the bed then make sure that Connal is watching the front and Jake is out back. Rogers is still sleeping on the couch in the front room. I swear to myself that my sweet girl will always be protected.

CHAPTER TWENTY-NINE

GUNNER

THE GUYS HAD TRANSPORTED MY BIKE TO MRS. RILEY'S HOUSE and by the time I make it to the safe house, I'm ready for the task ahead. The only thing bothering me is the possibility of having to kill Riley's parents if they were involved in this. I know she doesn't love them but the idea of it might taint our relationship.

I go down to the basement, thinking of the timing. I killed a Brother the night before and Deb has been moved to the room next to this, recovering after I burned her Northern Grizzlie ink off. I walk in to see Kennelly naked and either asleep or unconscious, I don't care which. I start tying off the ropes around his thighs. Once I decide he won't bleed out too fast, I unroll the pack of knives to start separating the skin from his shin. He's silent the first moment he awakens, then the screaming starts.

Within minutes, Jasper and Flint are in the room. "What the fuck, Gunner?" Flint asks in a low voice. "He's been talking."

"Don't give a fuck what he's been saying," I grunt out. "He scared my Sweetheart." I just keep on slicing meat off the bone. Flint takes a step further into the room.

"This is how I'm doing it, Boss." I glare at him. "Setting the *gold standard* for how all our Ol' Ladies are treated from now on."

Jasper reaches for Flint's shoulder and pulls him out of the room. Jas gets me, he's got kids to worry about. We can drop a flap of this fucker's skin somewhere, someday. That'll get the message across.

Kennelly starts screaming shit like, 'they weren't going to pay any more', 'they wanted her away from you', 'you shouldn't have touched her'.

Worthless bastard thinks I care what he says. He drugged, kidnapped, and hogtied Riley. No part of the rest of his short, miserable life will be pain-free.

"You want anything from him?" I ask, shooting a look back to Jasper. When he shakes his head, the only other thing I need to know is, "How many pieces for disposal?"

Once Jas answers me, I spend the next four hours with that sorry fuck. By then, I not only have shit on the Maddocks, but on two other officers in town. I am only relieved that the Maddocks were not involved in this attempt to take Riley from me.

And oddly enough, I like our sheriff enough to be pleased he's clean.

I shower at the safe house. I won't stain our home with this shit. The Brothers that will dispose of his remains are all in the living room when I emerge, the younger two keep their eyes on the floor like I'm the Boogeyman. They'll each take a bag and ride out different ways, all roads will lead to a wood chipper however.

I go to Mrs. R's home with the intent of bringing my Ol'

Lady to our apartment but one look at Ri asleep and I know that I will stay here with her as long as she needs. Seeing Rogers in a chair in the far corner of the guest room, I motion for him to leave. Clasping his shoulder, I say, "Anything you need, anytime, let me know."

"Just take care of her, Mr. Sorenson, just that," he says nodding at me.

"Gunner?" Riley whispers from the bed as he closes the door behind him. I proudly note she had slipped into her cut at some point. "Take me home?"

"You sure? We can stay here." I kiss her forehead lightly.

"Yes, I feel better." She looks up at me, pleadingly.

Nodding at her, "Let me help you get dressed then, Sweetheart."

Saying our goodbyes, I gather Riley into my arms. Ignoring her admonishments that she can walk, I simply hold her tight.

Once in our apartment, I walk straight back to the bedroom. Putting her down she strips naked quickly and I pull off everything but my briefs before sliding into bed next to her.

"The sheriff will call when they find him, right, Gunner?" She murmurs into my chest. I sigh, wondering how to answer. The sheriff has an APB out for Kennelly, and last I heard Michaels was shitting himself on how to delicately question the Maddocks about their involvement.

Leaning back to look into her eyes, my hands squeezing her shoulders so she knows this is serious. "They'll never find him, Sweetheart." Her eyes widen after a second, she stares intently at me then nods as if in response to some question she had herself.

"Are you alright?" She asks, cupping the side of my face, looking worried for me.

I don't know how to respond to her, so I slam my mouth down on hers. Riley has never, not followed my lead. She responds in kind, raising a leg to wrap around my waist.

"I went dark, Sweetheart, but you're my light and I was worried you wouldn't..." I start when I'm finally able to pull my mouth away from hers.

"Shhh, I understand why, Gunner." She takes my hand, laying kisses over it. "You promised you would never lie to me," she smiles sweetly at me, as if the dark in me is just a passing shadow. "Keep your promises and you'll always have me."

Sliding her hand down into my briefs, she starts massaging my hard cock. "No, Sweetheart, you need to rest." I try to dodge away from her, but she raises an eyebrow at me.

"I need you, Gunner. I won't be able to sleep otherwise. Please?" She lies back, spreading her thighs and bringing my hand up to her breast. My cock jumps, poking her in her thigh and she shoots me the smuggest smile I've ever seen.

Groaning, I duck my head down to her tits, holding them together to suckle both, until I ease a finger through her lower lips, spreading the gathering moisture.

"My Sweetheart's always so wet for me," I moan into her mouth. I quickly break away to grab a condom from my shelf. "Come on, now, get up on me."

I pull her onto my covered dick, gripping her hips; I help her find her rhythm. "Can you see if you can lick your own nipples, Sweetheart?"

Son of a bitch!

She can.

RILEY

Stretching out my sore muscles when I wake the next morning, I reach out for Gunner. Raising my head to look towards the bathroom since he isn't beside me, I quickly realize it was the smell of breakfast that woke me.

I pull on his discarded t-shirt from the night before and wander out to the kitchen.

"Hey, Ri, you're kinda ruining my attempt at breakfast in bed!" He leans over to kiss me while scrambling eggs.

"As if I could sleep through the smell of bacon!" I smile at him. "I've decided I'm skipping classes today, it's deserved after this weekend, right?!" I pop open a Diet Coke, and sit at the island, watching him as he works on breakfast.

"Absolutely, I have to stop at the clubhouse to see Jasper later, want to ride with me?"

"If you'll take me to the grocery store afterwards, the dinner is tonight."

"Riley! No one is expecting it. Fuck! After this weekend?" He looks really surprised but I want normal, not to sit around thinking about what could have happened.

"Text them that dinner's still on. I am fine and I want to spend time with everyone." He serves up our breakfast, pausing to text the group after I insist a second time.

I handle the dishes while he showers, surprised when my cell phone rings. Even more surprised to see it's my mother.

"What?" I don't have it in me to treat her with the respect she's always demanded of me.

"Riley, are you alright?" She asks, only slight pausing after my brisk answer.

"What? After your lackey hogtied me and kept me in a

root cellar for eighteen hours in the middle of winter?" My question is met with silence.

"Riley, I don't know what that...that biker has been filling your head with but we had nothing to do with this," she finally responds.

"Oh, so you never previously paid Kennelly to keep an eye on me?" I spit back.

"Well, of course, Riley. I mean we're gone so much and my mother insisted you be raised in that town she loves so much." She starts acting offended. "We're your parents. We just wanted you to be safe."

"You never wanted to be parents and now that I'm old enough to be independent of you, why don't we just keep it that way?"

"Riley, we'll be in town next weekend. Why don't you come to the house for dinner and we can clear the air?" She asks but I can hear her typing away in the background and know that she's already focused elsewhere.

"Is Gunner invited?" I ask. She can't think that I'd step foot in that house without him?

"Riley, you can't seriously expect that to happen?" She laughs. "My Goodness! The Blake's and their oldest son will be staying with us and you want a criminal in our home? Riley, we can talk and their son is an engineer of some sort. You two can talk about computers."

"I'm sure they'd just love the cut Gunner got me then! I plan on wearing it all over town, so maybe they'll see me when they're out shopping? It says 'Property of Gunner' in large letters across the back."

"I sincerely hope this is some sort of joke, Riley Jane Maddock!" Hmm, she sounds upset. "If the press obtain a picture of something like that, we'll be publicly ridiculed!"

"Alright, I've got to run. Let me know if you want to meet him, otherwise, I'm not interested in seeing either of you."

I turn back from the window to see Gunner standing in the entrance to the hallway. "Everything alright?"

"Yes, mother wanted to trot me out at the house next weekend. They've invited a friend and their twenty-something son." Gunner raises an eyebrow, crossing his arms. "I think I made it very clear that if you aren't invited then I'm not meeting up with them."

"Better get that ring for you real soon." He smiles, crossing to me. "Don't want my Ol' Lady running off with a younger man, after all."

Wrapping my arms around him, "I'm afraid you're stuck with me now, Ol' Man."

He kneels in front of me and quickly removes my underwear, treating himself to a second breakfast. I just barely stay on my feet, gripping his shoulders for the strength to stand while he licks and sucks my clit. The neighborhood must have heard my screams that morning. They'll be hearing them a lot.

CHAPTER THIRTY

RILEY

ARRIVING AT THE CLUBHOUSE SOMETIME LATER, GUNNER HAS me stay in the front room while he goes looking for Jasper. Moving behind the empty bar in the corner, I grab a glass and the spray gun for soft drinks.

"Oh! Just give me a minute." A woman shouts out from across the room. A blond woman I've seen in here before, a Girlie I think. She crosses the room with a large container of ice. "It comes out warm, so you'll want this!"

"Oh, thanks." I'm not really sure what the etiquette is with the Girlies. "I'm kind of a diet coke addict."

"I hear you, I'm down to two a day and that took a while!" Her eyes widen as she turns to smile at me and sees my cut. "Hey, that looks real good on you. Riley, right?"

"Yes, I'm sorry, I don't know your name?" She dumps the ice in the well behind the bar, scooping some into a glass for me. "Thanks again."

"I'm Betsy, been a Girlie a couple years now. I usually get breakfast for the guys and straighten the place up during the day. You ever need anything, just ask." She smiles shyly at me. "I help the Ol' Ladies coordinate parties they want to hold here also. Bree's wedding will be here in a couple months."

"Wow! I guess I didn't think of the clubhouse that way." I respond, thinking of Betsy in a slightly different light than how I considered the Girlies to be originally. I sit down, and fiddle with my cell as Betsy prepares the bar.

Probie soon comes out with more buckets of ice, "Riley! How are you doing? You alright now?"

Betsy's head spins around, surprised at the question, so I guess she doesn't know about my kidnapping. "Hi, I'm doing better. Thank you for helping the other day."

"I didn't do much. I felt bad I couldn't say anything when you came to the gate, and then..." He looks quickly to Betsy, and back to me, "Well, what happened later, I am real sorry. Anything I can ever help you two out with, I'm your man."

"Club business. I get it." I may not like it, but... "Hey, I'm sorry, I don't even know your name."

"Sorry, it's Mick." He wipes his hand on his jeans before reaching out to shake my extended hand. "Don't have a road name yet. Gunner in back?" He asks. I just nod, leaving him to stand there looking between Betsy and me. He finally goes for more ice.

"Betsy?"

"Yeah, Riley?"

"Any reason Probie looked so nervous seeing us together?" I keep eye contact with her.

She shrugs, "Look, you know I hook up with them. I definitely have my favorites around here. Gunner was not on that list, he just doesn't do it for me." She shrugs again, almost apologetically. "He figured that out pretty quick and didn't push it. He's better than some when it comes to stuff like that."

Speaking of the Devil, Frank walks in with some of his buddies. "Well, this is a motherfucking fine sight to see!" He bellows. "Betsy, why don't you bring that fine ass over here and keep us company?"

Seeing Betsy tense up and hoping I'm not making things worse, I pipe up. "We're talking just now, cool your jets."

I'm not sure who's more surprised, Betsy or Frank. Frank takes a step towards me but one of his friends grabs his arm. My 'Property of' cut is right in their faces.

As he's dragged off to a corner, she leans over, "Thanks for that, but now can we make it look like we're really having a heart to heart?"

One of his friends comes over, nodding to me, he orders a whiskey bottle and glasses from Betsy. "Hey, I'm Shade, heard about you." He nods to me. "Where's your Ol' Man?"

"Right here," comes Gunner's rough voice from the hallway. "Shade, Betsy, all good here?"

"All good, Gunner," Betsy's quickly replies. Having set up a tray for Shade, she slides it towards him while reaching over to refill my glass. Gunner orders a Jack as he crosses over to me.

Grinning at me, he leans into my ear as if to whisper. Instead, he lightly licks the outer shell before nibbling my earlobe. "Miss me?"

I wrap my arms around him and he slides in between my legs while leaning up against the bar. "I may have gotten Betsy in trouble with Frank, can we stay a little bit?" I whisper back. Shade has already headed over to his table and Betsy comes over.

"Betsy, I'm sorry. Did I make things worse?" I quickly ask.

"Nah, he'll get drunk and forget about it. Diamond or

one of his regulars will be around soon. I have to stay on the bar anyway. Thanks though."

"Betsy, I may need some help keeping this one out of trouble around here. You up for it?" Gunner growls, while smiling at me.

"Ha, seems like she likes her trouble big and grouchy! I'm not sure she'll need it but happy to keep an eye out for her." Betsy winks at me before moving away, pretending to be busy.

"She seems nice," I say shyly.

"She's pretty decent." He takes a sip of his drink. "You two talked a bit I take it?"

"Just a little." I smile back at him, "Don't worry, Gunner. Just you and me now."

He kisses the top of my head, "That's right, Sweetheart."

"Especially since I got my period right before we left home," I sass back, Gunner chokes on his drink. I see Betsy suppressing a smile as she reaches for a rag.

"Yeah?" He grunts, still clearing his throat. I nod at him. "Someday, Sweetheart," he says, rubbing my back.

"Are you disappointed?" I quickly ask him, surprised.

Betsy pours him another round, causing him to wait until we're alone again.

"I never thought about it before, and I want you to finish school, work, and live a bit cause we both know our lives will change after a child." He pauses and looks at me so lovingly. "But thinking of you, full with my child? See you holding our child? That *is* something I want, Sweetheart."

CHAPTER THIRTY-ONE

GUNNER

She kept saying I was rushing her, but damn I wanted her again before my Brothers showed up for dinner. She took her sweet time in the grocery store and preparing the meal once we got home. Guess I looked annoyed, cause then she took her sweet time sucking my cock to make it up to me.

I tried to keep a stern face while she was kneeling in front of me. She gave me that gorgeous smile of hers and slowly licking her lips, asked me to let my dick out to play while taking off her top off. Sliding her tits over the top edge of her bra, she flicked those peach tips till they got real hard. Finally, she moved her hands up to massage that sweet spot behind my balls then started in licking my length.

"I need that tight pussy, Riley," I moan after she's been working my dick in and out of her mouth a while. She leans back a bit, letting my head pop out of her sweet lips.

"But, I'm working so hard, Gunner," she says in between licks, looking up at me with those big, beautiful eyes as a wildfire spreads across her cheeks. "Can't I please swallow all your cum?"

Shit! I'd forgotten she started her period earlier. I'll wait till tomorrow and corner her in the shower cause there's just no way I'm going a week without her pussy.

"Will you do something extra for me afterwards, Sweetheart?" She nods up at me, working her saliva up and down my length with her silky hand. I smile down at her, rubbing my cock gently around her lips before letting her finish her work.

After she showers, I bend her over the bathroom counter and reach for the plug I picked up for my girl. Her eyes widen when I pull that and the lube out of a drawer.

"It's not that big," I say, working the lube around her tight hole with my thumb. "You keep this in until after dinner, got it, Sweetheart? Want to make it easier for you to take me back here."

She moans and nods while I slip the medium plug into her tightest hole. Kneeling behind her, I can't help but lightly nibble on her curvy ass. Flicking the end of the plug a few times, I stand and she arches back into my chest, her eyebrows knitted together as she studies us in the mirror.

Dragging my hand away from her breast, I cup her face while her wet hair drips down between our bodies. "What's going on up here, Riley?"

"That day at the car wash, Gunner," she looks at my reflection, unblinking, "Why?"

"Why what?" Riley knows I'm stalling so she just stands quietly in my arms.

"I was standing over you for a couple minutes, you know. Pissed I'd been sent over to deal with some kid having a meltdown until you looked at me. You weren't crying about your fucking SUV, Riley. That might have set you off, but

Jesus Christ, your eyes are so expressive," I wrap my arms tighter around her. "I felt something break in me, I wanted to take away all your pain. Can you forgive me?"

"Forgive you?" She looks confused.

"The shit I've done, the shit I will do? I need you so badly, the way you look at me like I'm everything." I drop to my knees, turning her to face me. "I will be better for you."

"You are everything to me. You are everything I always needed." She smiles down at me, repeating back the words she gave me last week, the words I crave. "I don't need you to change, just keep on loving me like you do."

"Always, Sweetheart," I swear, kissing her stomach and moving my hands to grip her ass.

"We've got to get dressed, Baby," she says as she tries to break my hold.

"Those assholes can fucking starve," I growl, making her giggle.

Dancing away from me, "Hey! I can't wait to meet Emma! I've heard so much about her."

She's left me on my knees. I can make grown men scatter with a frown but my Sweetheart laughs at me and leaves me on my knees, holding a dick that always seems to be hard around her.

Emma's cleared to drink again and Bree has a rare night off work so I've mixed some strong ass margarita's to keep up with Riley's theme of her homemade salsa and guacamole, as a snack before her enchiladas.

"Gunner! Stop it!" She keeps catching me going for the chips.

"Sweetheart, right now I get to munch on the chips or

you. Which one is it?" I'm laughing at her when the door buzzer rings, loving the blush that rushes across her cheeks.

The place smells amazing as I open the door to see the ladies heading up. Connal and Jake are maneuvering up a new flat screen, followed by Jas, Flint, and Vice.

Bree and Emma rush by me to greet Riley and after my Brothers get upstairs. Jas speaks up, indicating the sixty-five-inch screen. "This is from all of us, a housewarming gift." OK, maybe they aren't total assholes.

Connal and Jake lean it against a wall in the living room, just in time for Riley to get to them on her circuit of thank you hugs. I growl, taking her into my arms and making her laugh.

"Feeling left out, Big Guy?" She smiles up at me. Now that everyone's laughing at me, I release her to the flurry of collecting coats and getting drinks.

I've sat down to hundreds of meals with the guys. I expected it to be strained with the three Ol' Ladies thrown into the mix but it wasn't. It was just *more*—more laughs, new stories, a new audience for our old stories, and then the dinner itself.

Connal and I sat back and exchanged a glance as everyone had their first bite. We both knew that telling a person that someone is an amazing cook is so far removed from them experiencing it for themselves. Riley fidgets next to me, nervously waiting out the momentary silence for feedback. Tilting her head back, I kiss her.

We get a little carried away and when we look back to our guests, Jake speaks up. "Fucking A." He winks at my Ol' Lady, then digs back into his dinner.

"Sorry, Riley, we don't let him out much!" Connal contributes before starting on his portion.

The table descends into laughter and Riley looks back

up at me with such happiness and light in her eyes. She's surrounded by a family, friends, and my love—everything I wanted to give her that day we met. My throat tightens up and it's a little while before I can take a bite or say anything.

I look up to see Flint staring at me, waiting for me to focus on him. He gives me a nod, full of understanding and a thousand other things that men won't ever say to each other. Then his eyes flick to Bree before landing on Jasper. It must be a goddamn secret club because Jas nods back to Flint before repeating the motion with me. I see the way his eyes light up when he looks to Emma, and I know Riley makes mine light up the same way. Returning his nod, I then nod at Flint.

Jake is across from me and feeling his gaze, I look at him. He holds my stare a moment before looking down and quietly sets to finishing everything in front of him. Our quiet Brother saw our exchange and if I read the look in his eyes correctly, he wants in our secret club pretty fucking badly. Vice, as always, is oblivious as he reaches for seconds.

THE END, FOR NOW…

MORE BOOKS BY M. MERIN

Slate's Surrender (Black Hills Shifters Book 2)

Northern Grizzlies MC Series:

Jasper (Book 1)

Flint (Book 2)

Gunner (Book 3)

Charlie (Book 4)

Michaels (Book 5)

Betsy (Book 6)

Shade (Book 7)

Coming summer of 2019: Royce (Book 8)

Coming December 2018: His Touch

If you liked this, and even if you just want to leave constructive criticism, could you please leave a review? Alternatively, my email is merinbooks@gmail.com my Facebook page is M. Merin, and my newsletter is http://eepurl.com/dpHl9T

Thank you, M

Made in the USA
Lexington, KY
02 July 2019